Kid Stark

By Greg Tobin

JERICHO
STEELMAN'S WAY

Kid Stark

GREG TOBIN

DOUBLEDAY & COMPANY, INC.
GARDEN CITY, NEW YORK
1987

All the characters in this book
are fictitious, and any resemblance
to actual persons, living or dead,
is purely coincidental.

Library of Congress Cataloging-in-Publication Data

Tobin, Greg.
Kid Stark.

I. Title.
PS3570.029K5   1987   813'.54   86–29115
ISBN 0-385-23211-X

This novel is dedicated to the memory of
my father,
George Patrick Tobin
And to the memory of my mother,
Catherine Ann Tobin

PART I

CHAPTER 1

Here the mountains shouldered to the sky, ageless laborers eternally frozen in their silent work. Through the pellucid air, moonlight limned the peaks and created black shadows among giant boulders, in crevices and footfalls that rider and horse took pains to avoid. Joel Stark made his own trail through unfamiliar land, guiding his mount to the southwest where, he guessed, lay San Mateo and his best chance for a job of some kind and an end to the long ride. The clang of horseshoe on rock marred the otherwise flawless quiet. There was no echo. He thought it strange that he should be here at all, but he was too exhausted to be awed by the spectacle of the giant mountains.

Joel held the reins in his open palm. Through a close stand of juniper a faint wind touched him. The kerchief around his neck, a gift from Claire Thane, was wet from the perspiration of the day's ride and now felt like a cold noose around his neck.

He had ridden for five days without any rest to speak of. He and the claybank mare were hungry and thirsty; he had hoarded the contents of his canteen against the likelihood that there was no water for many more miles. But as horse and rider rounded the skirt of a basalt cliff, he saw a silvered bowl of grassland beneath the Peloncillos. There would be a river in the valley. He descended the last hill and reined up. The claybank stilled and awaited his decision.

Joel turned in the saddle and looked back at the moongilded mountains. He was sick of running but did not know another way. He was weary beyond mere physical exhaustion: his will to live had shriveled to a hard pit within him. Yet what choice remained to him? He buttoned his jacket to the neck. The mare blew thin clouds from her distended nostrils. He pressed his heels to her flanks.

After another hour he emerged from a finger canyon and spotted the improbable hovel sitting precariously on the side of the hill about a half mile ahead, with a soft orange light in the two small windows and a ribbon of smoke spiraling from the chimney. He was closer to San Mateo than he had thought. Perhaps this was a line shack. He approached cautiously.

At a safe distance he dismounted and called out: "Hullo there!" His left hand rested on the butt of his Smith & Wesson revolver.

At first there was no reply from the house. Lamplight refracted through the cracked glass windows. Joel waited, growing colder in the uncertain night.

Then a thin voice came from inside the hut: "Who're you, stranger? State yer business."

"Traveling through," the young man said. "Thought I might bunk around here for the night before going into town in the morning."

The door of the dilapidated cabin squealed open and an old man appeared in the light. He carried a shotgun and galluses hung from his waist. He wore only one boot and thinning gray hair sprouted in every direction from his large head. A yellow beard fringed his jaw, and the eyes, sunken darkly beneath the leather brow, were barely visible. Rheum dripped from his mottled nose.

"You carryin' a weapon, son?" the old man asked as Joel stepped forward. He did not relax his grip on the big twinbarreled cannon.

"Yes, sir. I'm wearing a pistol. Be glad to let you have a look. Don't want any trouble."

"Neither do I," the man said, his speech slurred. "Come on in. Slow."

As Joel entered, the smell of whiskey assailed his nostrils, mingling with the odor of sweat and soiled clothes. In the interior of the hovel broken chairs ringed a wobbly table and shreds of clothing lay on the floor among empty bottles and old china dishes and faded newspapers. A sense of impermanence, of mortality, welled up in Joel: he could smell it here in the close whiskey air, see it in the scraps of a man's life upon the floor.

The old man spoke up behind him. "Blue Dahlgren, stranger. Miner, prospector, and sometime rich man." He held out an unwashed hand.

The rider turned to shake hands with his host. "Joel Stark. Pleased to meet you."

Joel's smooth, thin face betrayed his youth—nothing he could do to hide it. He wore a flannel shirt and dusty workpants. Claire had also given him a leather vest, fitted to his lank frame, along with the bright maroon bandanna that lent a reckless look Blue Dahlgren did not seem to appreciate.

The old man regarded Joel through narrowed, watery eyes. "Seems I've heered that name before somewheres," he muttered, stroking the haggard yellow whiskers. "Sit down anyways. How 'bout a drink? You kin bunk inside or out—whatever you like."

"Nothing to drink, thank you—unless you have some water. I am kind of thirsty."

"Whiskey don't suit you? You be a churchgoer?"

"No, sir. Just haven't got a taste for the stuff." Joel moved to a threelegged stool near the stove and watched the old man pour from a begrimed pitcher of water with an unsteady hand.

"Cain't stand the stuff myself. Water that is. Here." Dahlgren snorted at his own joke.

Joel took the cup from a gnarled hand. "Thanks a lot." He gulped down the water and Dahlgren poured him another cupful. That too disappeared.

"You'll probably be wantin' grub too," Dahlgren offered unenthusiastically.

"No thanks. I've been chewing on hardtack all day. Sort of lost my appetite. Water's just fine, Mr. Dahlgren." Truth was, he was hungry as hell and missed the good meals Claire had prepared for him, even the trail grub his friend Henry Root had whipped together from nothing. But he could not take food from this man who plainly did not have enough for himself.

"Folks used to eat big at Blue Dahlgren's table— lots of 'em, including mayors and bankers, and they used to say, 'Mighty fine feast, Mr. Dahlgren, sir, thank you very much.' No more. Now it's just Old Blue by hisself. These days folks'd just as leave spit on me as talk to me." He took a big swig from his whiskey cup. "No, Blue is all alone now. The rest of 'em kin fry in hell for all I care."

Joel was too tired to reply. His supply of sympathy and compassion was all used up. He watched Dahlgren finish off the liquor and thought of his own father . . .

A loud crash shattered the morbid silence in the shack. In one swift motion Joel's revolver cleared leather and he kicked the stool away, taking the much-practiced stance, his gun hand whipping the cocked revolver up. His finger warmed against the trigger for a split second as he aimed at the source of the commotion. He did not shoot.

It was only an iron fry pan that had slid from a rusty nail and fallen on the black stove.

Blue Dahlgren's mouth dropped open, a pink hole ringed by dirty whiskers. He looked from the gun to Joel's face. "You're Kid Stark, ain't you?" he whispered.

Joel shook his head, suppressing a wry smile. "I've heard that before. People sure don't have much to talk about." He eased the .45 back into the crossdraw scabbard at his left hip.

Blue Dahlgren shuddered. He had let a mankiller into his house. A younker who had already claimed four or five lives, starting with a triple revenge murder up in Lamont, if rumor could be believed. Should of known better. Now he would pay the price for trusting a stranger.

He could not take his eyes from the young man's hands: the tapered ivory fingers that had, a few seconds ago, seemed as much a part of the weapon as the walnut grip or the grim barrel.

"Is you or ain't you?" Dahlgren persisted.

"Well, I'm a kid, I guess, and I'm a Stark, that's for sure." Color tainted his white cheeks. "I can see why some folks might call me that, but it's a funny handle, don't you think?"

He replaced the fallen stool. Dahlgren danced gingerly to the far side of the house, eyes locked on Joel Stark, wiping his hands futilely on his trousers.

"Not for me to think," the old man said. "All I know is what I just see'd—and that's good enough for me who's been around a bit myownself. You're the kid they been jawin' 'bout all right."

"Who's been talking about me?"

"I just listen to whatever drifts my way. You know —saloon talk and women's gossip and such. I never said nuthin', just listened, I swear."

"I'm not accusing you, Mr. Dahlgren. But I want to know who started this talk. Had to start with someone. Is there somebody in town asking about me?"

Dahlgren's black fingernails raked the yellow beard until Joel thought the old man was going to pull it out of his chin. Dahlgren considered and swallowed hard. "Not one in particular that I know of. Men are always coming and going around here. Mr. Stainback is the big wheel in this valley. Nobody'd put out any questionings without his sayso."

"Stainback. I've heard about him. He has a lot of business interests in San Mateo?"

"He owns the whole damn valley, you might say. He has mines—silver and tin—and a big cattle outfit and two banks and the general mercantile and three or four saloons and even a big cathouse. Nice place, I was in there once—"

"I'm looking for work. Think he might have something for me?" Joel asked.

"Work?" Dahlgren eyed his young visitor with an admixture of fear and curiosity. "You sleep in here, kid. On my cot. I don't mind the cold."

"I'll sleep up on the hill. I don't want to put you out of your bed, Mr. Dahlgren."

"Anything you say." The old man looked at the floor. "Listen, kid, about the job—pickin's is really slim hereabouts. All sewed up, sorta. Maybe you should try another town."

"I'll be gone at first light."

The saddle was a poor pillow but the only one he had. He had not yet gotten used to it and doubted he ever could. He would make a lousy cow hand. He wondered what sort of job he might be able to do for Mr. Stainback. He did not believe the old man's disclaimer. Surely there was something for him in this rich valley. A place to settle down, earn some money, then he would write to Claire, ask her to join him. Maybe he should not use his real name. Henry had told him that. It caused unwanted trouble. But Dahlgren already knew him. . . . Joel's neck and shoulders ached and he pulled the blanket up to keep out the cold. He closed his eyes tightly. The image of his father, fingering his mustache, hat clamped to his head, appeared for a moment and was gone. He tried to recall his mother's face but could see only Claire. What was she doing now? Was she thinking of him? He slept—

He dreams of a wide openness where deep shadows scar the land as night retreats before the advancing day. The bottomless sky is a bright lapis lazuli but there is no sun. Only prairie, no barriers either natural or manmade, except the far mountains which he can barely see from where he stands.

From the north come the riders, unchallenged. He cannot count them—four? six? ten? a score? A roiling black shadow, they seem to draw no closer. He hears the pounding of the hardrunning horses. He is rooted to the earth, the tall brown grass clutching at his legs. His lungs expand.

No wind, but the cold smell of spring, sodden with awakening life. No trees, no green, all is brown but for the distant purple mountains, slumbering. The sky remains cloudless. He is not in any place familiar to him, yet he is near his home.

He cannot move his feet, though the riders come on. The drumbeat of hooves upon the plain. He strains to see the men, sees a hat, a raised arm, a saddle, a horse's tail lifted like a guidon.

Of the earth but somehow apart from it, rooted yet soaring, searching. He turns and there he sees the house that his daddy built many years ago, smoke misting from the chimney and dispersing into the empty sky. Why is he here and not there? Where are mother and daddy? He cannot run to the house, cannot move a muscle. A chill shudders through his body —and yet it is unreal and is not there. He is only imagining it and all of this. Isn't he?

He turns again to the riders. Behind them, rising from the far horizon above the mountains, a boiling black cloud seeps across the sky with the swiftness of spilled coffee staining a fresh blue tablecloth. He can almost hear mother pushing back her chair and stifling a curse.

But, no, it is not that: it is a storm cloud, pregnant with pure cold violence. It will sweep across the plain and consume them all—riders and horses and house and his parents. He attempts to shout a warning, but he has no voice. He can only watch it happen. And it occurs with a suddenness that squeezes his heart to bursting.

The rain comes; then it is gone and in its absence is the clean heat.

The stormhead is transformed into a rolling ball of fire that torches the desiccated land. Talons of cindery smoke claw the sky, blackly obscuring his vision. Below, the flames destroy everything in their wake. Everything but the riders who remain a fluid shadow moving toward him, ever toward him . . . and he turns to see what has happened to mother and daddy and their house but no one, nothing is there. He is alone. The thick smoke pushes over him and he feels the heat of the fire on his face and he struggles to see, to breathe, to move, but he cannot.

JOEL STARK

✗ Ever since you can remember, you wanted to be a priest. Not like Father Orosco, the little Mexican padre at the old mission church where you and mother attended mass. You had grander ambitions than that. You thought that, like St. Francis Xavier, you would be called to convert pagan nations to Christ. A great Jesuit missionary: a black robe preaching among the unconverted Indians or the Chinese or the Africans. You prayed for the strength to follow this vocation and the wisdom to know what was false pride in yourself and true faith in Holy Mother Church.

Father Orosco encouraged your vocation through prayer and teaching. He saw in you what you saw in yourself: the capacity for knowledge and faith and good works. You respected his simple ways and how he had spent nearly his entire life among the heathen Navajo and Yuma peoples, bringing them the Gospel of Christ, baptizing them, instructing their children, and tenaciously battling superstitions and pagan practices that were unholy in the eyes of the Church. He had accomplished much. You wanted to achieve even more.

Yet—was this not the sin of pride?

You had read about many distant lands and strange peoples who had never heard of the True Church and who were waiting for the message, who required the Gospel to achieve salvation. The Church needed men to carry the message, and you thought you knew in your heart that you were one of these men. You knew what God's plan for you was. And it was a glorious plan.

Even in the dark times when faith was most difficult, when mother and daddy quarreled and there seemed no escape from the impotent pain of being their son, when love—for them, for yourself, for God —was a rare and precious and fleeting thing, you were certain that this great spiritual task would be your reward for suffering with and for mother and daddy.

When you wanted to damn them both, you remembered to pray for them instead. Though it was never easy.

The glory of God was a beautiful thing to contemplate: a mystery and a certainty, as indecipherable as the Latin Father Orosco had begun to teach you a few years ago. He had been a peasant boy himself, from a tiny village in Chihuahua, and he wanted to pass on to you his knowledge and experience, and he was the only example you had of the priesthood. He was a good man. For Christmas he gave you a copy of Thomas à Kempis's *Imitation of Christ,* which you have read and reread and tried to apply to your own life. It was a damnably difficult job to imitate Christ. Yet you vowed to do it to the best of your ability.

The glory of God. Life got in the way of a fuller understanding of this thing. You often thought, instead, of girls—those creatures who carried within them an attraction so potent it could make you forget any vow you had ever taken. You prayed to God to lift your soul and your thoughts to a plane of purity. Yet for the past few years girls have occupied your mind more every day. They possessed a beauty and a mystery that rivaled God's. Unapproachable, unknowable, undeniable.

How did Father Orosco live without a woman? Why did the Lord demand of His priests that they put aside marriage and children? When would the obsession pass? Or would it—ever?

Dreams of violence. Dreams of flesh. Dreams of freedom from the misery of life at home. You dream of becoming a man. Finally, becoming a man.

Daddy said: That priest doesn't know what the hell he is talking about. Don't let him fill your head with nonsense.

Daddy was not a Catholic and did not understand the truth of the Church. Mother made certain you were baptized, raised you to believe, took you to mass every Sunday and on holy days.

You said: Father Orosco is a good man, daddy. He has taught me a lot, and I respect him.

Man wears a dress. Never married. There's something wrong with that. It's not normal for a man.

What good would it do to try to explain the Church's teachings to him? It was something one either believed or didn't.

So you asked Father Orosco yourself one day when you went to the mission church to deliver some eggs mother had saved for the priest. He was grateful, invited you to sit with him in the chambers he kept in back of the church: a simple dirtfloored room in which he slept and ate and read Scripture and counseled his flock.

My son, he said in halting English, God demands of us many things. We do not understand the reasons for everything He asks us to do. But we must obey His will. As a priest, I know this. I sometimes wish I had a wife and children, but I cannot ever have these things, and I am content to serve the Lord as He has directed me. It is a great honor to be His priest. I do not ask for more than this.

Father Orosco's swarthy skin and wide face were shadowed in the darkness of his room, but his eyes glowed with the truth and power of his faith. His broad shoulders were bent, his robe loosefitting, soiled, frayed at the hem. He wore sandals that protected his callused feet but poorly. There was much to this man that you could not know unless you had patience enough to listen carefully to his words.

And his beloved church: it had stood for over two centuries, erected by a Spanish priest of noble lineage as a monument to the glory of the splendid conquerors of this rich and brutal land. The whitewash had long since faded and been stripped by rain and sun, but the graceful structure with the fragile bell tower and tall iron cross was still here and still sheltered the faithful who came from many miles to Sunday mass to hear the word of God from Father Orosco.

There was something unutterably beautiful about it all: the church itself, and the ancient burial vaults within that held soldiers and bishops and adventurers, and the priest's simple but unshakable faith, his dark eyes aglow with the light of Christ—and, it seemed, it had been put here by God to bolster your faith, to remind you of His love for you, among all His creatures.

You had been certain daddy was wrong.

But soon enough the certainties, the naive pieties, the protective cloak of youth were rent and discarded, leaving you exposed to fortune, naked, alone, and without faith.

CHAPTER 2

Joel awoke to the sweet aroma of bacon and biscuits. The bacon popped and spat in the castiron skillet on the other side of the curtain that separated his cot from the kitchen. His dream evaporated but left him shivering beneath his duncolored army blanket. He pushed himself up, swung his legs to the floor. In the semidarkness he slipped his legs inside worn corduroy pants, then pulled on his boots. He could hear his mother at work: the clatter of dishes, the kettle whistling softly, her footsteps between stove and table. Joel knelt and made the Sign of the Cross and said his morning prayer. Dear God, for another day I thank Thee. Bless and protect mother and daddy and guide my thoughts and deeds, in the name of Thy Son, Jesus Christ. Amen.

He folded the blanket and replaced it on the cot. He pushed aside the thin curtain.

"Good morning, mother," he said.

She said, "Clean shirt for you hanging over there." By the cold fireplace. The flannel shirt smelled clean, the sleeves felt stiff. Shifting his braces over his shoulders, he sat at the table. He ran his fingers through tangled red hair.

"Where's daddy?"

"He'll be in."

Eleanor Stark's back strained at the fabric of the plaid dress as she bent to open the oven. Joel noticed another strand of gray in her hair. She was thirty-six years old: shoulders slightly rounded, pale forehead lined, deep blue eyes somewhat dulled. She looked closer to fifty, an aging stranger who made him feel more of a boy when he was with her.

"Wash up, Joel. Breakfast is almost ready."

He went to the porcelain washbowl, poured water into it, and soaped his hands.

Bacon frying meant Saturday morning, the one day the Starks ate meat for breakfast. Saturday meant a trip into town for supplies and tailend chores around the house. He liked Saturday because it was the day before Sunday. On Sunday he and mother went to church and afterward Joel could read his books and complete school lessons for the rest of the day.

He watched her at the stove, then looked away. He looked at his own hands. They were not horned as daddy's hands were, or red and raw like mother's. He was faintly ashamed of this.

Eleanor turned the thick strips in the black pan. She said, "You're going into town with daddy today."

"Yes, ma'am." He dried his hands and came back to the table.

"Keep a close eye on him. I want him sober this afternoon. Too much work to do."

"Yes, ma'am."

"I know you don't like it. Neither do I. But that's how it must be."

"Why don't you ride in with us?"

She swept a blade of hair from her eyes. "When he decides not to shame me, I will ride into town with him."

"He doesn't shame you."

"He shames both of us. People talk. They know. I don't like them looking at me like I'm a martyr."

Two hen's eggs fried hard, two strips of bacon, and fried potatoes. She filled a mug with fragrant black coffee, lightened it with fresh cream. Joel shoveled egg and potato into his mouth.

Cullen Stark came in from the yard. "Morning, big boy." He went to Eleanor, touched her arm. "Got an extra egg there for me, mother?"

She served him without comment, then took her own plate to the table.

The three attended the meal silently. The boy sopped up egg with a buttered biscuit. The man shredded his bacon and sipped coffee. The woman, with an eye on each of them, ate quickly and without relish, for there was work to be done.

"I made a list of things," Eleanor said.

"Fine," Cullen said.

"We'll have to purchase on credit this week."

Joel stared at his plate, suddenly less hungry. He knew what was coming.

"And don't you dare touch a drop today," she said, spearing a cube of potato.

Cullen Stark gripped his coffee mug with spotted blueveined hands, opaque gloves of flesh, bony, tapered fingers with yellow nails, tobaccostained tips and thumbs scarred from lowburning matches. He dropped the mug with a crash, black coffee spilling onto the tablecloth. But he did not say a word and he did not look up. He bowed almost prayerfully over his plate. In the feeble sunlight that shafted through the window his bald spot shone whitely.

Joel knew the face of his father's anger, the cheeks red, the flanges of his nose white, his lips pressed bloodlessly together.

"We'll be back before noon," Joel said, wanting to believe it.

Eleanor went to clean up the coffee spill. "Don't treat me like this, Cullen."

"Man can't make a move around here without being watched like a hawk."

"There's reasons," she said. "After eighteen years."

Joel bit down hard on his tongue. He hated them both when they fought: his mother for her relentless inquisitions, his father for his cold silences.

"Leave it be," Cullen said.

"I just don't want you coming home drunk again." He did not reply. "Did you hear what I said?"

"I always hear you."

"Well you never say anything."

"Usually nothing left to say when you're done."

"Don't act clever with me, Cullen Stark. There's work to be done around the place—and you're bad enough sober."

"Leave it alone."

"I found five empty bottles in the barn the other day." There was a note of triumph in her statement.

"So?" He did not give an inch.

✗ "The boy hasn't had time to pick up your bad habits yet—thank the Lord. And I don't want him to."

"Leave the boy out of it."

"You're his father. He sees you near drunk every day. He helps me carry you to bed at night. He can't be left out of it."

Cullen looked at Joel. "Goddamn you, woman."

"Don't you curse me!"

"I'll talk any damned way I please under my own roof."

"Your roof? Who's been making mortgage payments from sewing jobs for thirty cents a day?"

"You know how I feel about you working."

"How you feel doesn't pay the rent. This farm is falling apart, and you—sneaking around with your bottles and smelling like a saloon and talking about feelings. Joel can smell it on you too."

"Shut up."

"I won't. Not until you get up on your own two feet and do something about this place."

"Shut up, goddamn it." Cullen Stark stood and planted his fists on the table. His moist gray eyes locked on Eleanor. She did not flinch. "I'll shut you up."

"Joel, your father is going to hit me."

"Don't tempt me, woman."

"Joel, he's getting mean. I may have to send you for the sheriff."

The boy blinked back tears. Damn them both to hell.

She turned to Cullen in bitter resignation. "Go ahead. Strike me. See if that will make you a man."

Cullen stomped out. The back door wheezed open and slammed shut. Footsteps on the gravel echoed back to the kitchen.

"That man will be the death of me," she said. "Eat your breakfast, Joel."

He pushed away the unfinished plate and drank some coffee, an eye on his mother. She held her face in her hands. He wanted to touch her but could not lift his arm. It was cemented to the table.

"I should have left him long ago. I could see it coming." She pulled back the loose strands of hair from her face and fastened them to the bun. "Promise me you won't treat your wife like this."

"I'll never get married," Joel said.

"Don't talk like that. You'll marry a fine girl one of these days. And I know you'll treat her right."

Eleanor rose and picked up her plate and cup. "Some women are just luckier than others. But I could never leave your father. He's really a good man when he's not drinking."

"Then why do you fight all the time? He isn't drunk this morning. Why start in on him like that?"

"I want him to stand on his own two feet. He could do it—if only he'd give up the drinking. I love him, Joel, crazy as that may sound to you. He's your father and you must love him too."

Joel wanted to be somewhere else.

Eleanor Stark put water on the stove to boil. "Go help him get the wagon ready. I'll clear the table."

When the boy went outside she stood by the window and watched him go to the barn where Cullen was. She was still there when they brought the wagon out, and her eyes were dry.

ELEANOR STARK

No one thought Eleanor Irons as pretty as her younger sister Meg. If this bothered her, she never allowed it to show. Eleanor became a woman quietly, almost before she knew it was happening, surprised more than pleased. The physical changes confused her. Nothing overwhelming—just what her mother had warned her would happen, the things her body did, the strange new feelings that stirred within her.

One day she would have her own life apart from her family, but the idea frightened her. All she had ever known was the cold, pious house of her stern parents who whispered between themselves that perhaps she would be better off in a convent after all.

Eleanor knew nothing of love. She had read a few novels of romance, despite her parents' proscription of such books. Her forbidden imaginings were vague. One day she asked Meg, who at sixteen had fallen in and out of love many times, What does love mean?

Meg said, Love is so sweet it can make you sick, darling.

How do you know when it happens?

It just happens. You'll know it, when you are ready and the right man steps in that door.

What if he never comes?

Meg shrugged her slender shoulders. Don't say

that, El. He will come. Every girl gets one chance at least. Sometimes more. But always at least one chance.

Eleanor Irons met Cullen Stark when she was eighteen. He was the nicest talker she had ever known; and he always dressed so neat, his shirts and coat pristine and perfectly fitted. In those days he wore a gray felt hat creased severely in the middle of the crown. She thought him handsome. She had never seen him on a cattle drive with alkalai and fieldstone dust staining his face, his clothing torn, his chaps splattered with mud and cow dung. When she met him he was flush, having concluded a successful cattle sale for a wealthy local man who owned a ranch in Texas and a major interest in the Union Pacific. He was ready to settle down. He had fought on the losing side in the recent war, he was not a Catholic, and he had little enough to offer by way of material prospects. Her family did not like him—for all these reasons—and made no effort to conceal their feelings.

Eleanor married him six months later with her father's reluctant permission, and she moved from Wichita to the farm outside Lamont he had purchased with a legacy from his dead brother. Her mother gave her a new leatherbound Bible; Meg sewed her wedding dress; her father said nothing.

Eleanor and Cullen made friends among the other families who settled in the area—ranchers, farmers, some townspeople. When Joel was born, Cullen had been so proud he rode from the farm to town at least ten times in three days to tell everyone he saw, to

distribute cigars, to buy drinks for any man who
pleaded thirst.

Their life was good, better than she had hoped for,
many times better than her parents had warned her.
But Eleanor was still young, and she had much to
learn.

June 7, 1875

Dearest Meg:

I am not much good at writing letters as you
know by now. I received your letter last month
and it has taken me all this time to reply.

If I had known Mother and Father were ill I
would have tried to come to Wichita, but it
would have been difficult because we have no
money now and things are bad here. But that is
nothing compared to what you have been
through with Mother and Father taking the
ague. You and James were so good to take care of
them and see them buried properly. I cried for a
long time. I just wish I had been a better daughter to them.

Cullen and Joel were very good to me during
my time of grief. You remember that Cullen lost
his brother years ago. Joel is a very smart boy, he
reads all the time, he reminds me of you with a
book in his hand always. You used to read so
many books. Cullen is doing fine but the farm is
in trouble because of the dry weather. In nine
years we have had only two good years but we
have faith in God that things will get better.

I cannot lie to you, Cullen is drinking some

and I must try to understand what a man feels in these circumstances. I am glad Joel is too young to understand what is going on with his father.

Please pray for us, just as I pray for you and your James. He sounds like a wonderful husband, Meg, and I am sorry I have never met him. He is the kind of man Father liked, I know. You are fortunate to have him. Why don't you have any children yet? You must want them badly.

I am expecting a second child in September but I am not very big yet—not like I was with Joel. I am worried that a baby will make it harder on Cullen with the farm going badly. Joel is such a comfort to us. He is a good boy. Mother and Father would have loved him, I am sure.

I don't know what else to say except to send my love to you, Meg. I don't want you to worry about me, I just did not want to lie or not tell the truth which is a sin. Please write to me again and tell me about your life with James and what is happening in Wichita, sometimes I miss it so much. Joel is going to school every day now, even though he could do a little more work on the farm, because we want him to get a good education. God bless you, Meg, and James too.

Your loving sister,
Eleanor

Joel's had been a quick delivery after only a few hours of labor. There had not been pain like this . . . something was very wrong. She had known from the beginning that it had not been right.

✝ The child was a little girl whom Eleanor and Cullen named Rachel. The time of Eleanor's carrying had been beset by illness and difficulty for the mother. Joel had been quiet in the womb and large, and though it had not been easy it was not like this.

Rachel had been small from the start, too small according to the midwife. Eleanor overheard her whispering to Cullen: There's a bad problem, Mr. Stark.

What is it? he asked.

The problem was, the baby's head was too large and the limbs tiny and lifeless and the spine malformed. Many problems. And the baby had been cramped and deprived of proper nourishment and oxygen in the womb.

Then she was a week late. The pain was something Eleanor had not expected. Long hours of intense pain, consciousness washing in and out and not hearing and muted shapes moving before her halfopened eyes. Once she did not know where she was or what was happening. But Cullen held her hand and talked to her and brought her back. She was in her own bed and the baby was coming and the pain, while it did not lessen, was different and there was the promise of release.

Rachel was born almost dead. She lingered for nearly a week. Long enough to receive her name and to be blessed by Father Orosco and for the neighbors to send food and words of comfort. And for Cullen to drink hard.

Joel was only eight years old, but he understood

that the oddly shaped creature in the crib was very sick.

She died one day and Eleanor held her. Cullen quit drinking until after the funeral. Joel would always possess the blighted memory of the helpless thing in mother's arms that had been his sister.

The years peeled away in layers to reveal why Eleanor had come to be where she was and how her life and Cullen's and Joel's had reached this point. Had there been another way? If there had, she had not seen it. Sometimes she looked in the mottled mirror over the washstand and cursed the face she saw there.

CHAPTER 3

Two long years of drouth. Cullen Stark, like other
subsistence farmers scattered beneath the Mogollon
Rim, had nearly gone under last year. A willingness
to go hungry some days had seen the Starks through
the worst of it. But this year held promise. A cold, wet
winter was behind them. Already spring was easing
warmth and life back into the sapped land.

On this morning in late March, the sky sagged with
gravid clouds, thickening the air with cool expecta-
tion. The sycamores, oaks, and black walnuts that
lined the riverbank thrust their greening buds up-
ward to catch the imminent rain.

Joel was eager to see and feel the fresh wetness of
spring, but he hoped it would not rain until after they
were finished in town. Then let it pour, let the planting season begin with a sign that God had not aban-
doned His people. Joel had not prayed so hard for
anything in his life.

The boy and his father boarded the old wagon.
Cullen sat erect with his hat snug and level, his shiny
shaven chin thrust forward as he jerked the reins. He
fit the wagon like a worn spoke. Joel sat forward next
to him on the creaking seat. The horse, a hipshot bay
mare of fifteen years, plodded along the familiar rut-
ted trail.

"Storm'll break before nightfall," Cullen said.

"We need the rain."

"Just in time for the corn and alfalfa. The feed crops'll take what they can get whenever they get it."

"Think we'll ever have a good year, daddy?"

"If we do it won't help us catch up much. We're in too deep. Take four or five good years in a row to dig us out." With nimble wrists, Cullen lifted the leather and gentled the mare along. "You need a new shirt, big boy," he said.

"Mother says she can patch up some of the old ones."

"They still fit?"

"Not too good."

"You're growing fast. Need a new shirt. Maybe a new pair of trousers too." Cullen touched his jaw line with the back of his hand.

"I don't know. Mother says I'll have to make do till next winter with what I've got."

"Well, what you've got ain't much."

"It doesn't matter, long as I have a couple of shirts for school."

"I wish I could do more for you, son. It's not that I don't want to."

"I know, daddy."

"Your mother and I both—we want a lot for you."

Cullen and Joel rode toward the advancing pewter clouds. Behind them, to the east, the sun shone weakly, powerless to halt the impending thunderstorm. There was a soft cool breeze and the smell of upturned earth.

As the road declined and twisted, about a mile yet from Lamont, the wagon groaned taking the turn.

"Twenty years come April," Cullen said. He let fly a bright brown wad of spittle that landed with a splat on a roadside rock. "Yaa, Mildred," he called to the old mare with a flick of leather. "Move on up."

"Twenty years what, daddy?"

"War ended. At Appomattox. I was holed up in the Ozarks. Didn't get word for three months. Bastards just all went home. Didn't bother to tell us boys out west. We fought that goddamned war for three more months."

"How come you don't talk much about what it was like in the war?" Many times Joel had asked Cullen to tell him about the war. But always his father remained closemouthed. Joel saw the cloud in his gray eyes and the taut veins in his neck. These were signs that Cullen was unwilling to say much else.

Joel wanted to know more than what he had read in books. Like Walt Whitman's verses about Mr. Lincoln and Mrs. Harriet Beecher Stowe telling about slave times and Edward Gibbon describing bloodbaths of Roman days.

Cullen rarely said more than a few words. Today was different for some reason Joel could not figure. "It wasn't no picnic, no glory run. I saw a lot of boys die—an awful lot of boys, some of them no older than you." Cullen rubbed his chin vigorously. "We were down at Galveston with Magruder when he captured it. That was in '63, right before things started to go sour. We were on the run after that. I made it out to Missouri with a bunch of Arkansas boys. We hid in the mountains for more than a year. Until the fighting was called off, like I said."

"Did you kill many men?"

"Men do things in war they would never otherwise consider. Me and my brother George were just boys. We figured we had to fight because it was the right thing to do. Turned into a bloody fiasco is what happened." He spat in disgust. "We left Crossville and put on our new gray uniforms with black piping and gold buttons and they gave us muskets and we waited to get into it. We got in soon enough. Scared—that's how I felt. George, though, he was afraid of nothing. He was mad for danger, George was. And a damn good soldier. Too bad you never knew your uncle. You'd of liked him a lot."

The wagon rattled over the road. The insouciant bay strained against the whiffletree, taking her own sweet time.

"George was a hellcat. You never saw a wilder boy. Looked a lot like you—with the red hair. Always had an eye for trouble, always in the thick of the fight. I remember the time he took on a horse thief in Junction City. He was twenty then, I was two years older. We'd just finished a drive of several hundred head to the rail yards. George knew this man from somewhere, East Texas, I think. Walked up to the man, shook his hand, if you please, and challenged him to a fistfight. Well, the damned coward wouldn't face George man to man. He called in four or five of his drinking friends. So I had to help George out of that one. We whipped them good. He took down three of them himself."

"You drove the big trails?"

"This was right at the startup of the trails. Old Jesse Chisholm—he was a halfbreed buffalo hunter, did you know?—had just took his first hidewagon up through the Nations to Kansas. Wasn't long before those Texans got in on it, though. Became big business—big herds, big men, big Eastern money. George and me needed the work after the war. It kept us fed for a few years, dressed nice. I met your mother in Wichita. Then George got himself killed."

"How'd he die?"

"Lousy fight over politics. Fellow stuck a knife in him and ran. Left George to bleed to death."

"Ever catch the man who did it?"

"She wouldn't let me go after him."

"Who?"

"Your mother. She had me married by then and made sure I didn't go out and get myself killed. I probably would of. But I had her, and George left me his money, more than I thought he had. So we came to Arizona and bought land. With a farm and a wife— too much of both for any man to handle proper. Then you came, pretty soon after."

"She's got a lot on her mind," Joel said.

"Always had a lot on her mind. Always let me have a piece of it too. Mother's a good woman, son, but be careful you don't marry a hardhead woman. Marry a girl who'll listen every once in a while."

"I told mother I'll never get married."

"Oh, you'll find some girl." Cullen Stark smiled dimly. "You'll make us proud."

"I'd never shame you, daddy."

"That's not what I meant. A man wants to leave something behind, something to show he has lived. A son, a grandson. It might sound kind of strange to you now, but one day—you'll tell your boy the same thing and *he* won't understand."

Joel looked at his father. Cullen's shoulders slumped as he held the reins in his big, hairfringed hands. His hat obscured his face. He wore a bushy red mustache that needed a trim.

The boy wanted to say, I'll never get married because I want to become a priest, but he knew it would only anger daddy and spoil the rest of the day they were to spend together. He did not want anything to ruin this time with daddy. It was all too rare that the two of them sat and spoke to each other like this.

"There are a lot of things I don't understand," Joel said.

"It's called growing up. Happens to everybody. Your mother'd say it never happened to me, but—" Cullen's eyes swiveled toward Joel.

"Daddy—" The boy swallowed dryly. "Why do you drink so much?"

"Not so much, compared to some men."

"But mother says—"

"She doesn't know what it's like, big boy. Sometimes I tell myself I'll never take another drink—and I mean it. But it never works that way. One of these days I'll quit—for good. I promise."

Joel looked away. Alongside the wagon trail the hills were eroded and brown and cold. So many questions remained unanswered. It made him angry—at his father and at himself. He heard Cullen cluck to the recalcitrant mare. The wagon jolted forward. Joel removed his hat and let the wind catch his hair and he gripped the sideboard with his free hand.

CULLEN STARK

He got out of the war with his skin and that was about it. The only good thing was George survived too. George had served in Virginia and the Carolinas while Cullen's regiment had fought in the West.

Cullen tracked George to West Texas and met up with him there in December 1865. George was working a big cattle outfit at the head of the Salt Fork. Ranching agreed with him: he had grown a couple of inches, put on some muscle, and acquired a beard since Cullen had seen him last. George was goodlooking, the kind of man women liked to be with, and he saw plenty of women in his free hours—even spending some time with a few on the ranch who were strictly off limits.

It was a fine reunion. George said Cullen had not changed much except he had started losing his hair. Cullen just smiled and said he was getting old. The war did it, George said. Cullen agreed.

The ramrod sized Cullen up and hired him and it was the toughest work Cullen had ever done in his life. But it was good to labor hard and put his mind to learning cattle work and sitting the saddle for endless, numbing hours in the cold of the West Texas winter—the winds gusting off the Llano Estacado and biting to the bone. A rough winter: keeping the cattle fed, watching over the cows carrying the spring count of new calves. A lot of earlymorning riding, toting hay through the snow, long hours in the cold, short nights trying to sleep through without waking, sweating from the nightmares.

George said it would take time to put the war behind them and he was right. Cullen looked up to George because he was bigger and stronger and faster with his fists and talked better. Cullen was broad in the chest, with overlong arms and not very tall, opposed to George's wellproportioned leanness, sinewy arms and legs. George was some girls' ideal type, while Cullen was at best a second choice in the looks and build department.

After some months Cullen started to put on some muscle and to look like a cow hand. The stiff new pair of Levi's pants he had bought soon became soft and worn, and his face filled out and was burnished by the wind and sun. He felt good—better anyway than he had for years.

His first spring roundup: awake before the sun, a bellyful of biscuits, beef, gravy, and lick, pots of coffee, then the backbusting pursuit of cows and calves, counting and branding and back out to the range to bring in more. Six hours of sleep and another day and another after that, till he came to think he might as well never step out of the saddle except to change horses. After the roundup, they celebrated with the other hands in town. They got drunk and nearly landed in jail and spent their paychecks with abandon, as if they expected plenty more where that came from.

Slowly, almost imperceptibly, Cullen started to put the war out of his mind. A lot of the other men on the ranch had been through it too—some of them bore visible scars and infirmities—and they talked about it. As long as you can get it out of your system, George said, you are doing good. So, with some talking and some drinking and a good new life close to his brother, Cullen started to sleep through the nights sometimes.

A year together, sometimes working till they were blind in the saddle from exhaustion. It was good for a man to work hard like that. It got all the kinks out, George said. He was always saying things like that to amuse and distract Cullen. And Cullen grew to love his brother even more and to depend upon him, to see the world through George's eyes.

George said, You want to stay here the rest of your life?

They had been drinking and the saddle tensions were melting away fast. They felt more relaxed than at any time in the previous twelve months. Another winter faced them.

Cullen said, I don't know. I don't even want to think about it now. All I want is to get drunk and maybe have a girl.

I know a nice girl, George said with a deep laugh.

The following year Cullen and George worked one of the first big northbound cattle drives. In September they rounded up two thousand head and lit out: twenty-five hands and one trail boss and one cook and two thousand head aimed for Junction City, Kansas. The Goodnight-Loving Trail had recently been established and they more or less followed it for the first sixty miles until they reached the Nations where they veered east and encountered the North Canadian River crossing.

When Cullen saw the rainswollen river his empty stomach knotted tightly. The herd moved farther east, looking for an easier crossing. There was none. They camped for two days, waiting for the river to go down. It did, some. Then the trail boss ordered the men and cattle across.

Cullen remembered every movement, every smell, every lap of water against his leather Cheyenne leg chaps. The sun was a golden disc hanging low, blinding him as he tried to outflank a wild bulge of steers that panicked as they hit the muddy water. He kneed his mount and reined hard to the left. The horse fought to gain a foothold, then lost it in the whirlpool created by the frightened cattle. Cullen gripped the reins in both hands, his hat pulled tight to the eyebrows. His vest became soaked and hugged his chest, made breathing difficult. He shouted for help but could not be heard by the others. Using his horse, he pushed against the skittered cattle to keep them a part of the herd—they could otherwise be swept away and lost.

Then a moving horn hooked his leg, and with a stab of pain Cullen was jolted from the saddle.

The crushing surge of water overwhelmed him, sucked him under. Cullen's lungs strained against the pressure. He thrashed toward where he thought his mount would be, but it was no longer there. Muddy water rushed into his nose and mouth and he tried to breathe out but could not. He fought the dead weight that pulled him down like an anvil tied to his leg. Suddenly his head broke out and he gulped air, but there was already water in his lungs. He went under again. His head was about to explode and the pain flushed through every limb.

He fought for as long as he had strength, then his body swept into the current and away. . . .

Cullen expelled the water from his lungs. Around him mewling cattle lumbered along the riverbank, dumb and unaware. Cullen saw George kneeling over him, soaking wet. Above, the slate sky hung low and heavy.

You're a lucky sonofabitch, George said.

You pull me out? Cullen asked.

Somebody had to.

Thanks.

Lost your horse and saddle. Boss didn't like that a bit.

Guess I'll learn to ride bareback.

Got to be a spare McClellan around. We'll fix you up.

Thanks, George.

Quit thanking me. Get up and let's find you a remount.

He had bellied up to death many times in the war, but it had never rattled him like this. Maybe it was the closest he had ever truly come: the swirling black water and the roaring in his head when it had nearly exploded. He learned from the other men that George had wheeled around and dived off his horse into the river among the panicked cows and plucked Cullen out before anybody else had had time to realize what was going on.

Awfully damned close, the others said.

The brothers never discussed the incident again, but it was always in Cullen's mind. Whenever he looked at George he remembered. For the rest of the drive—through the Nations and into Kansas—he was like a sleepwalker and he thought of little else.

CHAPTER 4

The wagon rattled toward town. Joel leaned forward expectantly. Though Lamont was not much, it was the only town he knew. It boasted two main thoroughfares: First Street, which ran north to south, and Lamont Avenue, east to west, forming a cross onto which the other streets were cut. Already he could see the people moving in the streets, some of them familiar to him even at this distance.

Joel attended school here five days a week in a house between the Methodist church and the pastor's home. Every time he passed it on a Saturday it seemed dead and alien to him—as if it were nothing, had no function except when he and the other town kids were inside taking their lessons, plotting against the teacher, wishing they were elsewhere.

For Cullen Stark the trip into Lamont was an escape from the farm, from Eleanor, from his failures. He looked forward to his weekly ride in as a prisoner looks forward to the daily walk in the yard. The closer the wagon brought him, the lighter he felt, the freer he breathed.

The road opened and the town spread out before them beneath a long decline. A collection of mismatched structures fronted the two main streets. The biggest and most substantial was the bank, a brick and fieldstone box with iron grillwork on the windows and a tall door carved from native mountain mahogany. Ahead, along Lamont Avenue, were the general mercantile, four taverns, a livery attached to the hotel, and a cafe that served the best blueberry pie in the territory. Once when Eleanor was sick in bed, Joel and Cullen had eaten a magnificent meal there: fried chicken and baked potatoes and carrots, all of it smothered in thick hot gravy. Topped off with pie and ice cream. Joel had enjoyed it so much that he sometimes guiltily wished mother bedridden more often.

"Get up," Cullen urged the mare.

They passed the old jailhouse that also served as a courthouse now that the law was better established in the county. Spiking out from the two main streets were narrow lanes on which stood smaller businesses and homes.

About three hundred people altogether now lived in Lamont. From its most prosperous days as a silver boomtown till now, it had shrunk somewhat, but the folks who clung to this modest place were determined to keep it alive, to make it work.

Rain clouds scudded across the sky from the north. Cullen said: "It had better hold off awhile."

Clucking his tongue, Joel looked far to the north where the mountains were now invisible in the gathering grayness. "Doesn't look too good, daddy."

"If worrying could bring it on we'd already be flooded out."

"I'm not worried."

"Not talking about you."

"Mother doesn't want us to be late."

"Don't bother over it, big boy. We'll do fine."

Joel shivered. He buttoned the neck of his corduroy jacket. It was a strange day: not nearly as warm as yesterday, as if winter did not want to release its grip on the foothills. And the rain. He knew it was coming and feared he and Cullen were going to get caught in it. They had brought their slickers, neatly folded in the wagon bed.

Cullen always carried an old .44 Colt's Walker with scratched rubber grips. He kept it oiled and dustfree, five chambers loaded, the sixth empty to prevent an accidental firing. Joel was alternately curious about it and scared to touch it. But his father had shown him how the gun worked and allowed him to fire it a few times. It was a heavy piece of iron, weighing almost five pounds, with a nine-inch barrel. Today it rode between them on the wagon seat, a piece of insurance against the unknown.

As they moved farther into Lamont, Cullen said: "The best way to handle trouble is to avoid it. That's why sometimes I don't talk back to mother."

"I suppose."

"When you get older you'll know. But I don't want you thinking I don't respect her."

Cullen looked straight ahead. "I want to do things for you, big boy—and for her."

Joel wanted to say, Then stop talking about it and do something—quit drinking so much and maybe then things would be better for all of us.

Cullen said, "Take the list to Mr. Blaine's. Our credit is still good there. He or Mrs. Blaine gives you any trouble, I'll talk to them myself. Come back to the wagon when you're finished. I'll meet you here." He pulled up near Blaine's general mercantile and braked.

He carefully adjusted his hat. "I won't be long," he said.

The rain pelted his shoulders. Joel shifted his feet, butting his back against the wagon. Fat drops hit the dust in the street; soon it would be a river of mud. The morning was not going right: he and daddy should have been halfway home by now. Joel had purchased the food and supplies and had been ready to go home for nearly an hour.

He was ready to start searching when he saw him.

Coming out of the Royal Pleasure, Cullen paused to consider where he was, stepped unsteadily off the boardwalk, then weaved slowly toward the wagon, holding his arms at his sides and trying to walk straight—but it was no use. Joel knew from long experience he was drunk as a bishop.

The boy lifted himself away from the wagon and started out to meet him. Then he heard the riders.

A deep rumble counterpointed the distant echo of thunder, only much nearer. Joel looked up and saw them coming into Lamont from the north, a dark shape—they rode closely together. Horses' hooves churned up mud and noise and sent townspeople running from the street. The rain came in cold silver sheets.

Joel shouted: "Daddy!"

The riders—six of them—bore down toward the

main intersection which Cullen was crossing. Joel ran toward him and reached him just as the snorting horses were upon them. He pulled Cullen back. Father and son stumbled as they tried to avoid the oncoming horses. They heard shouts and a single gunshot as they pulled away, felt the heat from the animals' lathered flanks and smelled the men.

Cullen and Joel fell, choking on rain and splattered mud and grit in the turmoil of men and horses.

Joel said, "You hurt?"

"Hell no." He groped for his hat, found it, and pushed it onto his head. Then he was on all fours.

Joel took his father's arm and hauled him to his feet. Cullen was not a big man but he felt almighty heavy. "Let's get home."

"Who were those bastards?" Cullen turned his head awkwardly.

"Don't know. Come on."

Cullen whipped his arm from his son's hands. He squinted through the rain in the direction the men had ridden. Their shouts came back at him. The street seemed as wide and wild as the Canadian River. What was happening here? Where was George? It did not make sense. His mind swam.

He moved with Joel across the street. Folks peered out at windows and doorways to see what was happening. Cullen muttered darkly.

"I got everything we need," Joel said. "We're ready to go back now. Mother is waiting for us."

"She'll likely want to kill me," Cullen said.

"Long as we get back safely, she won't care."

"Tried to tell you about women, big boy—wouldn't listen."

"I heard what you said."

"Hell." Cullen stopped ten yards short of the wagon. He held out his hand and collected some of the cold rain. "No fit weather for man nor— Wonder where those bastards came from?"

"It doesn't matter. Let's go, daddy."

"Run a man down like that. Coulda killed somebody."

"Nobody got hurt."

"Not the point—somebody coulda."

Joel silently prayed, Please, God, get us out of here now.

Cullen Stark lifted his face to the rain and let it splash on him. He went to the wagon, pulled the Colt's from the seat.

"No, daddy." Joel watched Cullen unwrap and heft the unwieldy gun.

Cullen planted his feet far apart and lifted the revolver to eye level as if he were aiming at something. Joel stood next to him, realizing for the first time that he was as tall as Cullen. He put his hand on his father's shoulder. Cullen spun to face him.

"Don't ever touch a man with a loaded gun in his hand."

"What are you doing? We've got to go home."

Then Cullen lowered the revolver. "Home."

"Please." This time Cullen heard him.

"All right, son."

Joel retrieved the oilcloth from the street where

his father had dropped it. Relief burned through him. The rain was falling steadily now.

Before they could step onto the wagon, the riders wheeled back around the corner, their pistols popping, their shouts louder even than the drumming of hooves on the sodden street.

"It's them," Cullen breathed.

"They don't want anything with us."

"By God, they'll get what they came for." Cullen still held the longbarreled Colt's. He lifted it again in both hands. He stepped away from the wagon. Joel was on the other side, his view blocked by the high seat.

Cullen shouted at the approaching men. "Who the hell you think you are? You almost hurt my boy and me, you—"

The six horsemen approached at a hard lope. In front of the Royal Pleasure they stopped, dismounted together, and loosehitched their mounts.

Joel moved out from behind the wagon to get a better look at them. He moved toward Cullen, tugged on his sleeve. But Cullen, an incongruous figure, boots planted in the mire, rain streaming from his muddied hat, did not budge. Like an absurd clay statue he stood there.

Laughter bubbled from the gang of riders. Joel saw that they were ranch hands, in open slickers and studded chaps, smallrowled spurs worn close to their boot heels. To a man, they possessed that pinchfaced, smalleyed look that said don't start anything with me unless you want trouble. Those eyes locked on Cullen Stark.

"Put the gun down, daddy." Joel moved behind his father and whispered, "Let's go home."

Through the pounding rain a man's voice shot toward them. "You want to test that cannon, mister?"

"The boy and me don't want trouble. Just want to know who the hell are you."

"Forgot my calling card," another voice answered.

"No joke! You can't just ride in here and run people down. I'm going to inform the law what happened."

"I'm informing you to shut your mouth and move out," one man shouted. The others laughed.

Joel watched Cullen closely. His temper had been simmering; now it boiled over. Cullen dropped to one knee and lined the Walker in both hands. Across the street the riders reacted swiftly. They moved away from their horses, and as one they too went down to their knees to present smaller targets.

"Daddy!"

Joel watched it happen, disbelieving, unable to stop it. He turned to the massed riders. He saw one man's pistol spit flame. Then another. The report from his father's gun exploded in his ear.

The gunfire stopped. Cullen brought the Walker to his chest as he fell facedown.

The boy grabbed the gun from Cullen's hands. Cullen rolled onto his side, his eyes open and sightless.

Joel lifted the Colt's and thumbed back the hammer. He shot once, cocked it again, squeezed the trigger. Then again and again. He emptied the revolver. On the opposite side of the street one man fell. Joel ran behind the wagon as bullets chewed into the wood.

JOEL STARK

When you finished your chores for mother before it
fell dark you ran out of the house to find daddy. You
were five years old with your pants cuffed up, just
growing into them. Your shoes were big, too, and
made running more difficult as you picked your way
across the furrowed field, tripping and swaying, in a
hurry. Seeing him silhouetted in the distance—so far,
it seemed to you—made you try to move faster.

He was there, waiting for you, arms out. Then,
lifting you to his shoulders, he carried you back to the
house, laughing, pleased that you had come to fetch
him.

You remember the pungent smell of him after his
long day outdoors plowing and planting and tending
the young crops. Gray mule hairs flecked his shirt
and you picked them off and he said that's how his
own hair would be one day: gray as a goldamn mule's.
And mother said, Quit cursing, Cullen, the boy will
grow up with a poor vocabulary if all he hears are
curse words. And daddy said okay because he wanted
you to have a good education and not struggle like he
did to read the simplest notice or newspaper story.

He seemed so big then, almost a giant. Even
mother did not look so big. Daddy blotted out a lot of
the sky when you stood near him, his shoulders so

wide, his legs strong, and his feet—the worn boots with chunks of mud on them made his feet seem even larger than they were.

In those days mother put you on her lap when she sat in the evening to read from the Bible, showing you words, telling you stories of ancient kings and warriors and prophets, and you listened with your mouth open to the delicious stories. Wondered how Jehovah put up with the follies and failures of his Chosen People for so long. Mother explained that all men and women were sinners and they only need seek forgiveness to be readmitted into God's great Heart. And how Jesus came to save us all from our sins by dying on the cross, rising from the dead after three days, and setting us all free.

Five, six, seven years old. You started school then in the clapboard house in town with twenty other kids who were never your friends. The other boys played together and raised hell in town and went fishing and swimming and all the things boys are supposed to do. You stayed home and read from the big Bible and other books borrowed from the school library. Every book you could lay your hands on.

Who needed friends when you had King Arthur and the Knights of the Round Table? And Robin Hood. And Ivanhoe. And David Copperfield. And Jesus. Mother always said Jesus was your friend.

Sometimes daddy worried about you, about how you did not get outdoors very often to play with boys your own age. But he was proud of you: how you could read before any of the other children and how the teacher gave you special lessons to keep your mind active and how you always said things that surprised him.

At night when you were in bed but not asleep he and mother would talk about you and he said, That boy will amount to something, I just know it. And mother said, He will be educated, Cullen, and maybe he will go to college and study to become a doctor, or maybe he will grow up and write books, or become a lawyer—maybe President one day.

That's when you became certain of your vocation. You would become a priest of the Church and carry the Gospel of Christ to the hungry souls. You kept it to yourself, though, and prayed about it and worried over it before you fell asleep and dreamed of the days when you would be a fisher of men and bring souls to Jesus. As big a job as you knew it to be, you never doubted God Himself was calling you into His service.

The Bible stories mother had read to you for so many years took on new meaning when you began to read them for yourself. Now you saw with deeper understanding the workings of God in the lives of men from the time of Adam to Moses to David and Solomon, through the days of the Captivity and the prophets who foretold the Messiah and the coming of the Kingdom. What a beautiful story it was! Jesus, then, fulfilled the promise of God to His children and proved His ultimate love for all men. And His Apostles preserved the Gospel, passed it to subsequent generations through the Church.

You were impatient to grow up, though that meant leaving mother and daddy and going out into the faithless world of men, a world which you really knew nothing about—except what you read in books. Faith, you told yourself, would be the ticket to success as an evangelist. Didn't Christ walk on water? Didn't Peter walk on water until he lost faith for a split second and fell? There was nothing more powerful than faith in God, and nothing could stop you if you possessed it in full measure in your body and mind.

The chores grew harder and consumed more time as you grew older. And daddy no longer seemed such a giant. He lost most of his hair except for a gray fringe. The farm got smaller when he had to sell off some of it to pay debts, and the rains were not enough in some years and in others flash floods wiped out the crops, and the last few years were especially hard on both mother and daddy. When she lost the baby she also lost him, it seemed.

That is when he started drinking more heavily and you knew it was bad from the way she lit into him—as if he were a wayward kid. It hurt you to see him like that and you did not know what to do about it. A test of faith, and you prayed for him and for mother and for the farm. But that didn't seem to work either.

Daddy had never gone to church, just you and mother, but after a while even she lost interest and you felt lonelier than ever.

You spent more time by yourself, in your dimly lit room with the curtain pulled or out near the creek bed behind the house. Nothing to do but read and think.

Started thinking about girls when you were about thirteen, confessed it to Father Orosco who warned against impure thoughts. There was one girl at school, Dorran Greenwood, a bank clerk's daughter. Never said more than six words to her the entire time you knew her but thought of her laughing eyes, her long legs and rosecolored cheeks. Did she ever think of you?

Now you are in deep trouble and must go home and make it there alive. Daddy is dead. There is no time to think. All of that is past.

Now you hold on to the wagon with bleeding fingers as the gunshots crash and the old mare runs faster than she ever has—in fear for her life. As you fear for yours.

Now the rain has come and it is too late.

CHAPTER 5

Before the smoke had been beaten away by the rain, Joel gained the driver's seat and the reins and wheeled the wagon into a nearby alley, then down a side street. He did not look back, did not stop to pull on his rain slicker. Skirted the northern edge of town, then plunged down a wide arroyo that took him into the hills. He ran the old mare all the way home. It took him a full hour.

"Joel! What in God's name—" Eleanor went to him, stripped his soaking jacket and shirt. "Take off your pants and boots. Where's your father?"

Joel pulled off his pants and boots, dried himself by the hot stove. His hair lay matted to his head. He watched his mother hang his wet clothes on a rope above the stove.

"You didn't leave him in town, did you?" she asked.

"He's dead," Joel said.

Eleanor turned her head slowly, her eyes narrow and cheeks more sunken than usual.

At first she did not believe what he said, she could not believe it. He told her how he had shot one of the men who had killed Cullen. The empty gun lay in the wagon bed covered with the oilcloth.

"You left him there?"

"I had to run. They were going to kill me."

"Jesus, Mary, and Joseph," Eleanor breathed. She brought her hands to her face. "This can't be. Dear God . . ."

"Mother." Joel went to her, put a hand on her shoulder. She was weeping quietly, tears visible between her reddened fingers. She seemed not to hear him.

Joel went to his room and removed his underwear. With his blanket he wiped his skin dry. Then he donned a new set of clothes—everything but his boots. He looked around. He took up the canvas bag his father had given him, the one Cullen had carried in the war. He stuffed an extra shirt and some socks inside. He surveyed his belongings: the dullbladed hunting knife went in, a length of rope, finally his dogeared Bible. He pushed the curtain aside.

She stood like Lot's wife, a white pillar of unrelievable sorrow. She had seen it all come down. He went to her again, tried to pull her hands away from her face.

"I must go to him," she said.

"Wait till tomorrow, when the rain stops. Look at me."

She did. "Are you hurt?"

"No. But I've got to go. Those men—they'll be coming after me."

A box of .44 cartridges for the revolver; a bottle of fresh water; leftover biscuits from this morning's breakfast; a chunk of boiled beef wrapped in paper; two tins of fruit. He stuffed it all into the canvas bag. It must have weighed forty pounds. It was all he could carry. He retrieved the supplies from the wagon, along with the Colt's Walker, and brought them inside.

Eleanor said: "Where are you going?"

"I don't know. I'll—" He looked away from her, standing there with bloodrimmed eyes, her hands clasped helplessly. Daddy was dead. Joel himself might be dead soon and that would leave her with no one.

"I'll write. I'll let you know where I am."

"We must bring your father home."

"I told you—the men who killed him—they'll want me. I can't stay here."

She heard him and yet she did not hear. He saw the incomprehension fade from her face, to be replaced by a dawning of recognition. "Why do they want you?"

"I shot one of them. I told you."

She breathed hard. "Yes, you said that."

"They will probably come here looking for me."

"The rain," she said feebly.

His hat sat dripping on the top of the stove. He took it up; it wasn't anywhere near dry. He shrugged into his slicker. "I know, but I've got to go."

"Your father—"

Joel clung to his mother with fierce energy. His own tears came hot and fast.

"My baby, my baby," she murmured.

"I can't stay, mother," he said. He pulled himself from her, sleeving away the tears.

"Who are these men?"

"I don't know. They just rode into Lamont, making noise, shooting off their guns. Daddy—"

"He was drunk, wasn't he?"

"That didn't have anything to do with it."

"If he hadn't been drinking it wouldn't have happened at all."

Through the incessantly pounding rain came the sound of approaching horses. She looked to the boy. He went to the window, but could see nothing. He picked up the heavy bag.

Then he was in her arms again and she held him with all her strength. He wept into her bosom.

"Here," she said. "Take this rosary." From her apron pocket she took her most precious possession.

"I can't."

"Yes." She pressed the beads into his hand and embraced him again.

Joel let the sobs out, flushing the tears. The bag hung from his shoulder, the revolver in his belt cold against his stomach.

He was out the door then, hugging the side of the house, listening for the riders. It was raining harder. It was raining too late to do any good for Cullen Stark or any of them.

Inside, Eleanor went to the front door, opened it to the lashing rain. The hem of her long skirt became wet as she stood there, and the wind washed against her face. Cullen was dead, and God she needed him so much. And what would become of her boy out there by himself? She was alone for the first time in her life and it frightened her.

Through the rain she made out the dark form of the oncoming riders. She looked around the room for a weapon. Cullen's old army musket hung from a peg on the north wall. Although dusty and unusable, she carried it back to the door and waited.

They were not long in arriving. Five of them moving through the storm. They wore dark slickers that concealed their guns. The lead rider held up his hand and shouted to the house.

Eleanor Stark gripped the old musket defiantly. "What do you want?" she called.

"The boy named Joel Stark," the rider said.

They knew his name. "You are the men who killed my husband," Eleanor said.

"It was an accident more than anything else, ma'am," the man said with incongruous good manners.

"Weren't nothing personal," one of the others added.

"My son was only defending himself and his father."

"Killed one of my men," the leader said.

Eleanor's legs were like water.

"Where do we find the boy?"

"I don't know."

"You're lying, missus. We won't harm him. We'll bring him back to town is all."

She did not believe them. "If he comes here I will tell him what you said."

"Missus, he's here—or he was here. We saw him light out, picked up his sign before the rain became bad. He's got to be here."

"Well, he isn't." She wore no shawl and felt the coldness of the rain penetrating her skin. If the musket could take a ball and a charge she would load it and shoot one of these men herself. "Get out. You killed my husband."

"Told you, ma'am—was an accident."

"You better go before there is another accident."

As she spoke the lead rider dismounted. The rain sluiced in a silver river down the folds of his dark coat and she saw that he held a rifle underneath. She took a step back into the dim warmth of the house. He advanced slowly at her.

"No more accidents, missus," he said. "I'm going to look around inside. If I don't find the boy we'll all leave peaceful."

He brushed past her before she could stop him. She smelled the wet and the rubber and the horse on him. She felt helpless as he searched the house. It took only a few minutes. Then he swept outside again and went to his horse.

She raised the musket and lined it threateningly on the man as he remounted.

The man brought out his rifle, all the while meeting Eleanor's hard gaze. He fired one shot into the heavy air. She wished only that the musket was primed and loaded and then she would show them the value of life and death. Her finger touched the trigger. The riders reined their mounts around and rode back toward town. Eleanor went back into the house and sat down, the useless gun across her lap, and wept.

PART II

CHAPTER 6

He needed a horse, he needed food, most of all he needed water. It was twelve days since he had run away. But he had no inkling of where he was or how far he had come—or whether anyone was still tracking him. He had left sign enough for a blind man to follow; his only advantage was that he did not know where he was going, so he had probably doubled over his own trail as he wandered in circles, heading south when he could, skirting mountains and keeping to wooded hills. Now his pack was lightened, his canteen empty. He had to find water soon.

He had slept poorly on the rocky ground last night. He was cold and afraid. He doubted he would survive in the wilderness. He wanted to go home, but it would be a long time before he could return to Lamont.

Lifting his face to the sky, he mouthed a feeble prayer—perhaps the hundredth time he had called upon God to aid him. He was beginning to feel strangely indifferent to his own fate, as if it did not matter whether God chose to abandon him or not. His meager life might not be worth preserving, after all.

The sun was well up and hit his face full and hard with its warmth. He swallowed dryly. To the west lay

a blue range capped with snow. He wished himself
on a mountaintop where he could spy the rivers and
streams that he could not locate on the ground. He
shouldered the war bag and turned southeast.

By late afternoon Joel was dizzy. He stumbled on.
Something pulled him forward, and he let instinct
take over. It was thickly wooded at this elevation:
dark pines, tall oaks, greening sycamores. He walked
through the heavy underbrush that tugged and tore
at his trousers. His legs were stiff and heavy, and the
bright sunlight hurt his eyes.

An hour before dusk he sighted another distant
copse. Cottonwoods? Water? He did not allow himself to hope too much. At least night was coming and
though it promised to be cold, he could rest. He
moved slowly, impaired by fatigue, and achieved the
trees before the sun fell. There he found a lazy rill,
cold and clean. He drank long, held the water in his
hands like gold, and splashed some on his face.

Joel sat for a moment and tried to think, to plan.
His mind was crippled, almost broken, and he aban-
doned the last shred of hope to which he had clung
like a frayed rope. He lay beneath a tree.

He awoke with a deep hunger. His belly had been
full of water which helped him sleep for several
hours. He emptied half the canteen and refilled it.

Joel removed his hat. His hair was dirty, plastered
to his skull, and he felt an intimation of whiskers
growing on the underside of his chin.

Food. How and where to get it? The Colt's Walker
weighed against his hip. If he could find game and
shoot it—but he was not confident of his skill with a

gun. It had been luck—most decidedly bad luck—
that he had killed that man in Lamont. Two men
dead, including daddy. As his stomach ached hol-
lowly, a shrunken empty sack, he felt sick.

Kneeling beside the stream, he poured water on
his neck and tried to order his formless, directionless
thoughts. He was alone and close to starving. It
would do no good to lie down and give in—not until
he had given himself every chance to survive.

That day he followed the newfound stream farther
into the hills that bordered the Mogollon Rim, looking for game.

Joel picked a place where the water rippled over a
wide but shallow bed of pebbles and hunkered low
beside a tree and waited, not sure what he might
encounter. He slowed his breathing and held himself
motionless. Within an hour he felt himself part of the
tree and the earth and the stream, and he was reminded of James Fenimore Cooper's savages who
lived with the land, became brothers with the trees
and rivers and sky.

The wind blew across his face and filled his lungs.
Time slowed. The many sounds of the land became
clearer and closer and more distinct. He was not
alone. Joel did not move a muscle.

He heard daddy say if he was patient he would be
all right. Almost heard daddy's voice—but it was
more like a part of his own brain talking to the other
part. He felt his blood running warmly through his
veins. Daddy said be careful with the gun and never
shoot unless the target was still and well within

range. His heartbeat slowed. He must have patience is all.

Patience. Two hours passed. Three hours of thirst and hunger. Patience, he told himself.

Just before dark he heard movement through the undergrowth. Then a coon about twenty inches long, with a ringed tail at least that length, shuffled to the water. It sniffed the air suspiciously but went to drink, its tail twitching.

Crouching about five yards from the animal, Joel eased the gun barrel up. The shadows shifted as a soft breeze eased through the trees. He held his breath and squeezed the trigger. An alarum of shrieking birds startled him more than the explosion and he slumped down, trying to make himself smaller, invisible.

The coon lay with its bloody head in the stream.

Joel waited until his own heart stopped its violent pounding before he rose and went to the dead animal. The sight sickened him, but he picked it up and sat by the water and carefully skinned it with his knife. He cut off the tail to save—for what, he did not know. Then he gathered dry sticks and built a small fire. He gutted and cleaned the animal and held it on a stick over the fire.

It tasted fine, if tough and stringy. It was enough to answer several days' hunger. He drank some water when he had finished his meal. He threw the carcass into the fire and watched the bones blacken. At nightfall he slept.

* * *

At first it was insubstantial, like a dream. Then he smelled the fire and thought he had not extinguished it completely. Then he remembered that he had thrown water over the fire and it could not be burning. Sunlight slashed through the budding tree limbs over his face. He sat up.

The fire burned fully but no smoke was visible. A coffee pot sat among the red coals and a strip of meat over the flame. A man sat on a fallen tree trunk, a rifle across his lap.

"Coon is lousy meat," the man said.

The features of the man's face were hidden by his hat brim. Joel raised his head slowly, to get a better look. It took a few seconds for him to realize that the man could have slit his throat as he lay there asleep. He hadn't, but he still could.

The stranger turned the green stick to expose another side of the meat to fire. It was an economical movement of the wrist. Joel saw the man's dark hand. He wanted to speak but his throat was dry and tight. The food and coffee smelled good.

Finally, Joel brought himself up on his elbows. "Howdy," he said.

The hat came up a few inches. The man said, "Fine morning." The quiet syllables betrayed nothing about him.

Might as well enjoy a meal before he kills me. Joel shifted to his knees and reached for the canteen. He took a quick swallow, his eyes on the man. Then he went to the stream and refilled the canteen. When he returned to the fire he put his face close to it to dry. The heat trailed into his nostrils, mingled with the bracing air.

" 'Spect you're hungry?" the stranger said.

"Yes."

"Pour yourself some coffee." He held a battered tin cup.

"Thanks."

He took the first sip as if it were poisoned, resigned to the outcome, but it tasted all right. He wondered what time it was. "How long have you been here?"

"Came up before dawn. Heard some shooting and smelled your smoke last night. Not good to show yourself so plain hereabouts."

"I didn't know anybody else was around."

"There's always somebody around. Apache bucks on the scout, drifters, every brand of bad man. Things haven't simmered down as much as the government says they have. You're lucky it's me that found you."

Joel thought about that and realized it was probably true. Better this man than the gang from Lamont, or some renegade Indians. Still, he was not so sure about the stranger. He talked friendly enough, but what did he want?

The man removed his hat and said, "My name is Henry Root."

"Joel Stark. Pleased to meet you."

"Stark?" He said it as if it meant something. He came over to Joel and held out his hand. It was black and hard. He had a powerful grip but did not squeeze Joel's hand overly hard. He had nothing to prove.

Henry Root stood well over six feet in worndown,

workedout boots, his black hair cropped close to the skull and graying at the temples. Thin, probably from spotty eating on the trail, with square shoulders and those big hard hands. His blunt nose overshadowed a thick mustache that was carefully trimmed. He had eyes the color of whiskey, open and clear, steady and unafraid.

He wore black trousers, a blue work shirt, and a loose jacket with stubbly fringe. The flatcrowned hat was banded with hammered silver scallops, a fancy touch to the otherwise utilitarian cowboy garb. Instead of a belt gun he wore a big knife.

The only Negroes Joel had ever seen were the ones who lived in Lamont: the blacksmith and his son, a storekeeper, a man and wife who operated a laundry, some men who worked ranches in the area. The odd thing was, Joel did not recall ever looking any of these people directly in the eye. Perhaps it was because his contact with them was so infrequent.

Root was lightskinned. He remembered daddy once describing a man he had worked with as "high yellow," and he supposed that fit Henry Root. Only his hands were truly black.

"Where you going to?" Root said.

"Don't know for certainty."

"Like me. I been lots of places and probably be to lots more before I'm done."

"I've never been anyplace," Joel said.

"How can that be? Weren't you born someplace and lived someplace with your folks?"

"Yes."

"Then you've been at those places."

"Same place. Lamont."

Root looked Joel over closely. "Lamont. That's where I heard your name. Somebody got killed up that way."

"My father."

"And some other folks too."

"The man who killed him."

"Don't have to talk about it if you don't want to. I can understand you feel bad about it."

Joel thought nobody could understand. And he surely did not want to talk about it. Who knows but Henry Root might take him back to Lamont, turn him in to the law. Joel felt a twinge of unease. He turned away and busied himself needlessly with his bag. The heavy Colt's was in there, loaded, if he required it again.

The Negro turned to the fire, lifted the coffee pot out, poured himself a fresh cup. It steamed whitely in the frigid morning, wisps curling into his face.

HENRY ROOT

Oddly, only his hands were truly *black,* and if it were not for that he might have been able to pass for white. But he never had faced the opportunity or desire to do that. His own folks sometimes eyed him with jealousy and suspicion because he was so yellow and his eyes so light and his lips not so thick and he did not talk with a Southern plantation drawl. He even knew how to read a little—enough anyhow to get by in the cattle business and occasionally to peruse a newspaper whenever one floated into a line shack.

But, yellow or not, however black his hands were, whatever shade his eyes, he was just another nigger to most whites.

After a successful drive to eastern Montana, he had been refused a room in a hotel, and not even the fanciest in town but a rundown hostelry on the farthest edge.

Henry Root said to the proprietor: Mister, I am as clean and honest a man as will ever cross your threshold and I do not understand why, if I can pay for it, I can't have a room. I'll pay extra for a hot bath. And I'll pay for it all in advance.

The hotelkeeper was dogged, sweat shining over his lip and on his chins. He said: We've never had a nigger stay here before. Don't know what the others might say.

What others? I'm sure you run a respectable place, but I have not seen many high society roomers about.

Listen, if I let you stay this once then every boy that rides through town will want to stay here. It's nothing personal. I'm sure you're a right fine boy— and clean to boot. Just can't set a precedent on this thing.

This is not a court of law, mister. All I want is a bed for two nights and I'll be on my way. Believe me, I'll not spread tales of my good fortune across the territory.

No use. Henry spent those two nights in a cold bed roll on a hillside outside town. Not the first time nor the last that he would settle for such accommodations. The thing was, he could never get used to it and he would never give up asking for what was his by rights. After the war there were supposed to be no more barriers. So, what was wrong?

Henry was smart enough—and you didn't even have to be smart—to know that it was color, pure and simple. Fourteenth Amendment or no. Henry was an all-out-or-nothing sort of man; it was against his nature to hold back. Yet he held back when it was necessary to keep the peace. And sometimes even that did not work.

Best time he could ever remember was when he hired on at the big Jerusalem outfit in southern Wyoming, worked there for four years through every season and every condition—some pretty rough— and with every type of man, rose to top hand at top

pay responsible for less shit riding and more important duties.

At the Jerusalem, Henry began to reap the rewards
of long years in the saddle. As top hand he worked
directly under the ramrod, a bantam name of
Schuldiner, for whom fairness was inborn and tough-
ness as much a part of him as his hands or feet.
Schuldiner wanted only to get the job done and was
merciless to slackers, though kind enough to those
who worked at his pace, which was fast and rough.
He smoked little brown cigarettes endlessly throughout the day and drank every night. He had died hard
in the saddle some years back, but he had never
slowed down.

Schuldiner once said to Henry: Any sonofabitch
that sticks his nose in where it doesn't belong is likely
to get it bit off. So I don't. But I just want to tell you
this once, anybody gives you grief on account of your
color, you tell me and I'll take care of it quick like.

The ramrod blew smoke from his beak nose. You're
a good hand and that's all that matters.

There were times when another man said or did
something to make Henry feel uncomfortable, but
Henry never said anything to Schuldiner. He was
satisfied to know that the ramrod was on his side—in
case there was ever real trouble. Henry did not talk
much, to Schuldiner or anyone else. Always there
was his color, always the veil between himself and
the others, always the suspicion on the part of the
white hands that some of his black could rub off on
them.

That made Henry laugh aloud. The idea that it

could rub off like ink or bootblack. He wished it could.

Winter hurled ten-foot drifts upon the Jerusalem and the men sought shelter in the rude bunkhouse around the glowing iron stove. Henry Root sat among them and listened to their complaints and jokes and tall stories, but said nothing. Often he thought about his mother in Kansas—she was still alive in those days, well past seventy. Outside the wind battered the logs of the bunkhouse.

One morning Schuldiner came in, an iced cock, and shook the cold from his feathers. He had been up before first light. He was that way.

I want three of you boys to ride with me to the west fence. Forty head trapped there. We'll haul some hay out to them.

Henry went for his woollined coat and scarf and gloves. No one else seemed eager to abandon the stove. A dozen pairs of eyes dropped to the floor.

Don't care which of you it is. Draw straws if you want. But two of you get your asses out to the stable and saddle your ponies—now!

He marched to the door, Henry two paces behind. The four men saddled their mounts and tied sleds of hay to their saddle horns and rode out toward the west fence into the face of the blizzard. The storm had intensified since the morning and bit at the riders' faces and stung the horses.

Schuldiner shouted above the wind, directing the men and struggling with the burdensome bales of feed for the stranded cows. The wind whipped away his words and the snow obscured him from view. Henry provided the link between Schuldiner and the others; he too fought to keep the cold and wet and wind from pounding him back.

The two other riders were not so committed to the enterprise. The iron stove was a warm memory. Who needed this icy ride to nowhere just for the sake of a few head—all right, a few dozen?

The snow was a white wall so thick you could barely see a foot in front of your face. Henry Root attempted to keep Schuldiner's back in sight, but it was almost impossible. He heard the other two grumbling to each other below the wind, and he knew he had better watch them.

Schuldiner led the men to the fence line, and there were the cattle, bawling, their noses steaming, milling in close, cold quarters. At least three were dead, frozen stiff, one standing where it had died, a grotesque statue. The ramrod called to the men to circle with the hay bales among the cattle. It was difficult to move even a yard in the snow which came up to the horses' flanks.

Move! Schuldiner shouted hoarsely into the storm.

Henry brought his mount around with a quick jerk and a knee to the ribs. The other two hands reacted more slowly—too slowly for Schuldiner.

You men better be quicker than that, or lose a day's pay— The angry words trailed off into the howl of the swirling snow.

On a day like this—

Why doesn't the nigger—

Likewise their replies were swallowed by the wind.

The job done, Schuldiner ordered them to ride north to scout for any other Jerusalem cattle that might have strayed into the area.

The two hands balked.

Not likely, one said. We're riding home. Cows be damned. He reined around.

The other looked at him, then to Schuldiner, undecided. Finally he turned his horse.

Get back here, goddamn you both, Schuldiner cursed.

Root watched the confrontation unfold, the gnawing fear in his gut. He put a gloved hand on the butt of the .45 in his hip scabbard.

Schuldiner lashed out with a piece of rope, cutting the second rebel's face. The man screamed. The first man turned in his saddle, reaching for his booted carbine. He lifted the gun and fired a quick shot that hit Schuldiner in the left shoulder.

Henry shot the first cow hand out of his saddle, then lined the revolver on the second man's chest.

Schuldiner, stunned and bleeding, said, Thanks, Henry.

To the mutinous rider he said: Now, you get your friend back onto his horse and ride ahead of us back to the barracks.

The man did as he was told this time.

But that was the end for Henry and he knew it. He had shot a white man, and no matter that Schuldiner was on his side it was over. When, a month later, the weather broke he left the Jerusalem and rode south.

That had been a few years ago. In between there had been infrequent jobs. A spring roundup in Utah with a halfassed outfit he was glad to leave, a long dry summer, more riding, an autumn gather in northern New Mexico that paid better than average but did not turn into a fulltime situation, a hard winter with not much to eat. Drifting from season to season. He thought of trying his luck in Mexico. Maybe he still would one day. But he had some friends in Tucson who might know of something better. That is where he was headed next.

As long as he kept riding, kept looking, he would find a job. Henry had learned not to hope too much. There was no point. But he must work. That was all he had.

CHAPTER 7

Joel ate the pork strips, drank more coffee, and stole a look at Henry Root who did not bother trying to make conversation. The boy managed to fill his belly —and dear Lord it felt good. The last time he had eaten a real breakfast was the morning daddy was killed.

Henry Root seemed to grow bigger and more menacing as Joel stared at him. It was the strangeness of him more than the way he moved or what he said. He was filling his pipe.

"Ginny Gal. Best tobacco in the world," Henry said. "Want to try it?"

Joel had never smoked. He said, "Sure."

Henry took a spare clay pipe from his saddle bag. He tapped in a pinch of the golden tobacco: Virginia Girl, it was called. Joel knew that much. Henry lit the pipe and passed it to the boy.

Joel drew too deeply, and the smoke burned his lungs. He coughed violently. Henry sat back and watched him.

"Take it slow. Taste it. Don't try to smoke the whole damned bowl at once."

The second pull went in a little easier. Joel tried to look casual about it. The smoke curled into his face and made his eyes sting and water.

"Like a couple of Injun chiefs," Henry observed, propped comfortably against his saddle, enjoying the smoke. The two of them were silent for a while, concentrating on their pipes.

Finally Henry Root spoke again. "You fill our canteens, we'll be ready to move out."

Joel hesitated. Was it right taking orders from a Negro? Should he trust this man? Daddy had always said you couldn't be too careful. Then again, Mrs. Harriet Beecher Stowe had shown in her book how Negroes were real people with a sense of honor and responsibility, if her writings could be believed.

He reminded himself he had nothing to lose that he had not lost already, except his life, which at present he valued as worthless.

Henry carried two canteens. Joel filled them and his own. Henry by that time had cleaned up the campsite and covered all sign of the fire. He took up his rifle. He said, "You coming?"

"Where?"

"Out of here. I thought you were on the scout."

"I am."

"Then you want to ride with me?"

Joel fingered the canvas war bag. He wanted to trust Henry Root, but he had known him for only a few hours—not really known him at all. He needed time. There was no time.

"I'll go with you," he said.

He followed Henry to where a blue roan and a tall claybank were picketed about twenty yards from the camp. The animals greeted him with a curt snort. Henry said to the claybank, "Easy, girl. Want you to meet Mr. Joel Stark. He'll be riding with us for a spell."

Henry Root fastened a singlerig California saddle on the claybank and a doublerig on the roan for himself. Joel would ride the claybank. The Negro threw the heavy saddle and tightened the cinches with such skill and ease that showed Joel this was a real cowboy, no mistaking. One horse to ride, the other a packhorse with an extra saddle just in case. The movements were—the whole man was—efficient, economical.

Joel wanted to say something but stopped himself. It would not be polite, and it was none of his business. That was one of daddy's favorite sayings: "None of your business."

"Give me your bag," Henry said. Joel handed it over and Henry Root tied it with his own saddle bag and blanket roll in a tight bundle that would ride the cantle behind Joel. It was a neat business and Joel admired Henry's practicality. He imagined the man had spent a lot of time in the saddle.

It was still early morning when they rode down the hill onto a stretch of hardpan that promised no comfort. The claybank stepped carefully through scrub and around the big rocks strewn everywhere. The country was more desert than not, something Joel had never seen before, only heard about.

Secretly he hoped they would encounter a renegade Apache who had busted out of the San Carlos reservation or a Mexican whiskey peddler traveling the same trail, but also feared such a meeting. He held to the reins tightly, his palms moist. He feared Henry Root too.

To the southeast the great Chiricahuas rippled against the sky, distant but palpably large. Joel remembered the story of Hannibal and the elephants, which he had read in history class. Hannibal had outsmarted the superior Roman army by pushing his men and his elephants over the Alps to Rome's back door. He had eventually lost the war, but he had conquered the Alps.

Henry's saddle creaked musically, the animal's bit jangling, the stirrups bumping against the flanks of the horse. Sometimes Henry Root hummed a tune which Joel did not recognize but guessed was a Negro hymn. These sounds mingled with the occasional screech of a lowflying bird that looked like a crow.

"One of these days—" Henry Root's voice startled Joel. "A man will ride through here and see houses and towns and even farms."

"I thought this was Indian land."

"Not no more. It's nobody's land, just the government's. Oh, they'll find gold or silver or something—some folks already have—and get rich and buy up big parcels and build it all up grand."

"Who do you mean?"

"Rich white folks. Won't be no room for the Indian or anybody else."

"You know any Indians?"

"Knew pair of 'em once. Crow boys. Smart and tough enough, both of them. They were just trying to get along, like everybody else. Rode with them for a while." He volunteered nothing further.

"You have folks anywhere?"

"Don't know. It's been a long time since I've been back."

"Where do you come from?"

Henry Root turned in the saddle and looked at Joel. "Why do you ask?"

Joel flushed red. "Just curious, I suppose."

"Curious as to who this nigger is and where he comes from and what is he up to—is that it?"

When Joel summoned the courage to look at him he saw Henry's smile. "That's it."

So Henry told his story and Joel listened and it helped pass the time riding and sitting by the fire at night. Hearing Henry talk kept Joel from looking over his shoulder all the time.

"That big old Walker is going to weigh you down," Henry said. He pushed another greasewood stick into the fire. The moon was high and they had stopped early on a foothill near a small cave. Henry thought rain might come again.

Joel said, "It is a heavy damn thing."

"Here—" Henry held out a smaller revolver with a shiny blue barrel and walnut grips. "It's a Schofield-Smith & Wesson. Takes a lighter charge in .45 caliber. Try it."

The gun, with an oddshaped, short handle, was much easier to handle than the big Colt's. Joel grasped it expectantly.

Henry said, "Like how it feels? It's a single-action, no fancy stuff. It's been good to me."

Joel considered. The Walker had been daddy's—it

was a part of the family, almost all he had left of daddy.

"All right," he said.

"I'll give you a hundred rounds with it," Henry said. He got the cartridge box from his saddle bag. He took the Colt's and hefted it, examined the workings. "Fair enough?"

"You going to show me how to use this thing?"

"Maybe we'll do some target practice tomorrow, after we put some more miles in. I got the feeling somebody's not too far behind on our back trail."

Henry reached into his saddle bag and came out with another prize: a tooled leather holster. He showed Joel how to wear it on his belt so the revolver rode butt out on his left side.

"Handier that way," he said.

Joel had never worn a gun scabbard before and had never planned to. So many things were different now: guns and horses and Negroes and men pursuing him, daddy dead, mother and home far behind, and ahead a day on the trail to be followed by another and another after that.

Joel slipped the revolver back into its holster. The metal slid against leather.

"You've got long fingers. That helps," Henry said.

"Daddy showed me how to shoot some."

"You're going to need to learn more, son—and fast. You've made some people angry at you."

"I guess so."

"I'm just telling you to be prepared."

JOEL STARK

The only certainty is death. Salvation, the promise of reward and renewal, cannot be known or proved, only believed.

In your mind you return to the mission church remembering what you learned there, but it is difficult to believe anymore. Faith is an alien idea. The saints of old had died with faith flowering in their hearts. Somehow they had the strength to endure the trials of the flesh and prevail. In God's eyes they had triumphed while other men, earthbound, struggled meanly toward nothingness.

The musty darkness, the weakly flickering candles, incense lifting through the dense air; Father Orosco's thick, gentle words, the alien tongue of Mother Church; Thomas à Kempis had written: "It is good that we sometimes have griefs and adversities, for they drive a man to behold himself and to see that he is here but as in exile, and to learn thereby that he ought not put his trust in any worldly thing."

Still, words—even such eloquent words—did not prepare you for what had befallen. And had you been stupid enough to believe that they would? The pieties of youth had become moot. Was that where the fault lay? In your own ignorance and pride?

The death rattle of gunfire in the rain, daddy

slumped in the mud, the mare whickering in fear, the cold touch of the wagon wheel as you held it to stand, and even colder the trigger of the gun that had killed a man. Freedom from these memories would mean freedom to live, perhaps even to approach salvation. But it would take time for the memories to pass. Seventeen was not too early to seek a beginning, but too soon to find the end.

Jimmy Grueke was a neighbor kid, a year younger, probably your only school friend. At least he talked to you sometimes and once in a while the two of you went swimming in the creek that ran along the north line of the farm. Jimmy's father owned the land on the other side of the creek and he had had no better luck than daddy over the past few years.

Last September it had rained for two days, swelling the creek. The two of you met there and had a few good days of swimming, and for the first time you talked to another boy about some of the secret things you thought about only alone and at night.

I saw my sister naked last night, Jimmy announced one day.

Since you had no sisters you were denied this privilege. You said nothing.

She was mad at me.

Why?

She said nobody was supposed to see her till she gets married. I don't know what it matters.

Jimmy dove from a ten-foot rock. His pink body knifed through the clear, hot air and sliced into the brown water. You followed him and he tried to push your head down. You fought him, but he was stronger and he finally relented.

Haven't you ever seen a naked girl? he asked.

You tried to imagine every square inch of flesh, every mysterious detail. No image came to mind.

No, you said.

My father says she better get married soon or else it doesn't matter a damn if she parades naked through the town. He says she hasn't got anything the whores on Second Street don't have. That got her even madder.

I always thought your sister was pretty.

Pretty damn stupid if you ask me.

Jimmy challenged you to jump from an overhanging tree limb about twenty feet high. You did it and were scared every inch of the climb, but the fall into the water was exhilarating.

I like Dorran Greenwood, he said. She's a good looker.

Jealousy flared, unwelcome, and you lashed out, pushing water into Jimmy's face. You jumped on him and shoved him under and held him there by the shoulders. He flailed at you, tried to escape your grip, but you pressed, kept him under for a full minute. Only then did you relent. He came up, gasping, angry.

What the hell did you do that for? he sputtered, crawling toward the bank.

I'm sorry, you said, not meaning it.

You like her too?

I think she's real nice.

Why didn't you say so? I won't talk about her if you

like her. It's not like you two were married or something.

I guess I do like her a little.

Hell, if you're willing to kill for her it must be more than a little.

I didn't mean to hurt you, Jimmy.

He lay on the bank beneath the tree. You lay beside him and looked up through the heavy branches into the patchwork sky. It was hot, still, and humid. Soon the school term would begin and you would see Dorran and the others. Maybe this year would be different. You and Jimmy had become friends. It was a start.

It's hard to talk to girls.

Hell, I talk to my sister all the time. She doesn't give a damn. Girls aren't as smart as we are, anyway.

I don't believe that.

It's true. Just ask my dad. He knows all about girls.

When you had confessed your sins Father Orosco said, You must guard against temptations of the flesh.

The priest had said the same thing many times, and each time it made no more sense to you than the last. You had not asked Jimmy to share his illicit secrets. How could you avoid temptation when it came upon you uninvited? Like the thief in the night.

Yet, if you were committed to your vocation to the priesthood, you must learn to put these thoughts behind you.

Father, sometimes I can't help it. There is a girl at school—

You must pray more. Do you say your rosary?

Every night before I go to sleep.

That is good. Trust in God.

Yes, Father.

The priest absolved you and for penance assigned five Hail Marys. It was a much less severe penance than you had expected.

You did not understand the quality of the sin, nor the logic of the punishment. You prayed for knowledge, humbled yourself before God and Father Orosco, and waited for an answer.

That night you dreamed you were swimming in the creek with Dorran Greenwood, both of you naked.

CHAPTER 8

"There are other towns besides Tucson, probably safer ones too," Henry said.

They were riding along a deep dry arroyo, away from the mountains. It was early morning and their breath misted before their faces.

Joel had slept poorly. He was unsettled and not fully awake. He had only the vaguest idea of what he might do in Tucson if that was where he was headed: try to find work, a place to live, a means of survival. He said, "I'm not sure."

"Might think of changing your name," Henry suggested.

"No." Joel thought Henry was exaggerating the infamy his name enjoyed since the shootings in Lamont. Henry had said some people were calling him "Kid Stark" and claiming he had killed four men.

"Just a thought. If I knew who you were, other folks are going to know too."

"They don't know anything about me."

"You got to realize, people talk. They talk more than you like them to. Hell, they have little enough else to keep their feeble minds occupied."

"Why would they care about me?"

"You killed a man, like it or not. No matter they

shot your daddy. That makes you a mankiller and that is plenty enough for them to talk about."

They were making good time over the flat brown playa, heading southwest toward the Gila River. The farther they got from Lamont the better he felt, though he thought of his mother with growing anxiety. If folks were talking about him, it would all come back to her and she would have to live with what he had done. She might be in danger now, and he could do nothing about it.

He turned to Henry who was gazing across the clear expanse that lay ahead. "Even if they talk—what can they do to me?"

"Son," Henry said, "you got to understand what I'm trying to tell you. It's not just the talk. It's the way they talk. Then there's somebody who will listen to that trash and decide to do something about it. And whoever is on our back trail will listen out for word on you. That's what you got to be careful of—he's going to try to track you down. It's for your own safety that I say you should change your name, go somewhere they don't know about you."

"I think I understand what you're saying. But I'm not afraid."

"Lord sakes, boy—it's not a matter of afraid or not afraid. It's a matter of staying alive!"

Joel said, "Who's on our trail?"

"I can't know for sure. Maybe one of the cowboy crew from Lamont."

Even as the sun climbed higher and grew warmer, Joel felt a chill within.

Henry said, "Don't be downhearted. Happens to

every man at least once in his life. Just happened to you earlier than most. You got to face it head-on. Whatever you choose to do, stick to it. Right or wrong, you got to make a choice."

"I don't want to die, Henry."

"Don't none of us want that."

"It's a feeling I have."

"Don't worry yourself about no feelings. If you hear gunshots, that's when you start worrying."

"I had a dream the night before they killed daddy. I never thought it meant anything."

"Most likely a coincidence. A bad dream never killed nobody. Your daddy's dead and you can't have another. You got to be a man all by yourself." Henry reined up. "Let's water the animals. All this talk must of made them plenty thirsty."

The day waned. Joel, sitting the claybank, held it a length behind Henry.

The black man turned to check on the boy. Joel was a gaunt figure who looked older than seventeen, yet infinitely younger. He was marked with death, would either give it or get it.

The claybank snorted and tossed her head. Joel put a calming hand on her neck. They were riding over a stony stretch that was hard on the horses. As much as they tried to make it easy on the animals, this route was a rough one—necessary to leave a less easy trail to follow. Joel wore his new Smith & Wesson in the tooled holster on his left hip. He touched it again to reassure himself that it was there. He longed to practice with the weapon, to get the proper feel for it and gain more confidence in his ability to use it.

* * *

Before dark, Henry left Joel at their cold camp by a sheltered stream to scout their back trail. All day he had been disturbed by the instinct that the men following him were getting closer.

Joel waited, chewing on dried beef strips, angry to be left behind, afraid to be alone; but he had resigned himself to Henry's superior experience in these matters.

The Negro rider returned after three hours. By that time it was full dark and colder. A tattered scrap of cloud drifted across the quarter moon. Joel started when he heard Henry several paces behind him. Henry led his horse into the camp and picketed it next to the claybank.

"What did you see?"

"Not a hell of a lot," Henry said. He paused, squatted on his haunches to gain eye level with Joel. "Best I can put together, it's one man less than a day behind us. Don't know any more than that."

"How do you know that much?"

"I can see pretty far, even in the dark. We got any more of that hardtack? I'm like to starve if I don't eat a decent cooked meal soon."

Joel gave him a strip of the beef. "What are we going to do, Henry?"

"Let me finish my supper first. Then I'll come up with a real smart plan."

He sat back as Joel tended to the horses. The boy vented some of his anxiety by giving Henry's big gelding a thorough rubdown and watering both animals. He wanted to move, wanted something to happen—anything but this enforced sitting on the trail. He was sick of it all and wanted it to be over with so he could go home.

Henry smoked his pipe, and Joel came back to the campsite wishing for a fire. But it was inadvisable to build one tonight with the rider so close behind.

Finally Henry said, "We'll split up tomorrow."

"Why? Isn't it more dangerous that way? Together we can fight him off."

"Not necessarily, boy. If we split up it'll confuse the bejesus out of him. He won't know which one to follow. I don't fancy our chances with him. I'll be honest. I kill a white man here and I'll never work in this territory."

"We're not looking for trouble. It's him. He's the bad cousin. We're just defending ourselves."

"Tell that to an allwhite judge and jury. If I pull the trigger, even in selfdefense, it's free passage to Yuma for me."

"I wouldn't let them do that to you, Henry. Besides, why does anybody have to know? If we finished him out here and buried him, we could ride away clear—as long as we didn't tell—"

"Things don't happen that easy. Someone'd likely miss him, start asking questions, get the law involved. It could get ugly pretty quick."

"Damn it, why?" Joel breathed through his tears.

Henry chewed his meal. "I know it ain't right. But I'm thinking of you. It's the best way." He explained his plan. "Way I figure it, I'll strike out west a half mile from the river—very visible. You take the claybank down this stream to the river, slow and easy, cover your tracks that way. He'll have no choice but to cut my sign. Then you get across the Gila the best way you can. There ought to be a ford a few miles to the east. That'll put a lot of distance between him and you. You take your time, you'll be safe as a baby."

"What if he catches up to you?"

"He won't. He's in for a hell of a long ride before he knows he's chasing this old nigger." Henry chuckled as he prepared his bedroll. "Did I tell you about the time I almost got lynched in Dakota? I suppose I didn't—not something a body likes to remember, much less jaw on. Vigilantes were looking for a gang of rustlers and couldn't find them. Found me instead —alone and dead tired—and they figured I'd do. Rode that claybank there five hard hours. Outrode all of them. They must of been drunk anyway, because they didn't keep up the chase."

Joel said, "Didn't it make you mad?"

"Not so much. A man of color can't afford to get too angry."

Joel pulled the blanket to his neck and soon heard Henry's rhythmic snoring.

Fine dry snow covered everything for as far as Joel could see. Henry boiled coffee over a small smokeless fire. Joel observed the rolling gray storm clouds. It was late in the season for snow, but it was not uncommon at this elevation.

"Drink this," Henry said, pouring the coffee. "We have to get moving."

Joel said, "I've been thinking, maybe I should ride

with you after all. The two of us should stick together."

"Don't go thinking on me. It's better the way I planned it."

The horses had rested and fed and were ready. Joel and Henry saddled them and secured their bed rolls and provisions. Henry erased as best he could the remains of the campfire. Then he led both horses to the stream. The animals nosed away the sluggish layer of sleet to get to the cold water. Henry then moved them farther downstream, leaving a profusion of sign that would take their pursuer a while to decipher.

Henry and Joel mounted. "This is where we say adios, son."

Joel reined the big claybank around and put out his hand. "Thank you, Henry."

"You'll be fine if you keep an eye on your back trail. We'll meet up again in Tucson. Ask around. You'll be able to find me pretty easy." Henry's amber eyes shone. "It was good riding with you."

"You too."

"Remember, stick to the stream. And don't be afraid to use that pistol if you have to."

The black man kicked his horse into a lope down the hillside. Joel watched him until he was a small figure, black against the fresh snow that hugged the earth. He felt for the butt of the Smith & Wesson at his hip.

COREY LOGUE

The rain was the worst of it. Soaked to the soul, a man had to ride through it anyhow to get where he was going. For four days Logue had ridden through the rain after the kid who had killed his best friend, Stan Prol. He had been ready to give up, but he kept going and the rain had ended. Logue aimed to extract some revenge—for himself and for Stan.

The eyes that pinched against the nose were sharp and farseeing. Had to be for the work Logue did with cows on the wide range. He'd done his share of gun work, too, when called upon. Mainly clearing the boss's valley of squatters and the occasional raiding savage who had not heard of the safety and comfort available on the reservation. The fingers fit around a revolver like a hawk's talons, natural and right, and with the feral eyes combined to make Logue an accurate shooter from whatever distance his weapon could accommodate.

In the case of the Stark kid, he would get right up close where the revolver could do its damage properly. Put a bullet in the boy's skull. But something was bothering Logue. The boy was no longer on foot, as he had been out of Lamont. He was on horseback and he was not alone.

Both animals were in good shape, well cared for,

and making good distance. His own mount, a paint mare, was tired; he had driven her too hard for the first few days and the rain had given her a cold in her lungs and now the snow would keep her back. He should rest her for a day and wait for warmer weather and feed her good and give her a chance to recover before pushing on. It might be worth it in the end.

This killing business was not as easy as he had anticipated. The boy had been on foot, armed only with an old Colt's Walker, and Logue had every advantage. The boy's mother had failed to throw him off the trail. The rain had done a better job of that at first.

He only wished some of the others—even just one —had ridden with him to avenge Stan. Prol had been a friend to all of them, but they were scared that having killed the boy's old man they were in trouble enough. They had ridden out of Lamont for their home range and not looked back. Only Logue had stayed on the boy's trail.

He considered the terrain ahead. The mare was watering greedily at a cold rivulet: meltoff from the winter snows. He refilled his own canteen, then picked his nose. The two riders had been smart, choosing a rocky trail that was more difficult to track than the softer lowlying route at the base of the hills; the higher ground made for a harder ride, but a safer one for the pursued. Smart—he had to give the kid some credit.

Logue had never claimed to be smart, just persistent. Twenty-seven years old and already the hair was thinning badly on top of his head. He wore a hat all the time, a fine gray Stetson that he had paid twenty dollars for. Even inside, in the bunkhouse, in the boss's office, in whatever tavern he might frequent whenever he was in one place for a time. It was his only vanity.

He wore a stained cotton work shirt and dirty Levi's denim trousers and scuffed boots. He rolled his sheepskin vest and lashed it onto the saddle. Too warm for that heavy thing; anyway it made him sweat and smell like a goddamned sheep. His beard was over a week old now, a light blond fuzz that barely showed; mainly it was itchy.

Corey Logue had not started out bad; he had not turned out bad. Only rudderless. This business of avenging Prol was the first clear goal he had pursued in a very long time. He remembered only one similarly clearcut intention in his life—that was to get out from under his father.

Logue had grown up—after a fashion—in New Mexico, on the old man's big ranch. His brother Gary was to inherit the spread: Gary was a hard worker and smart and older than Corey by five years. It was only right that the eldest son should inherit. But it wasn't right the way the old man treated Corey, like he was a hired hand. One day he got sick of it and cut out, riding west, not knowing or caring where the hell he was going as long as it was a far piece from the old man and Gary.

He drifted out to Nevada and tried mining but that was no good, then he made it as far as California and found ranch work and hated it but stuck to it because at least it was not the old man telling him what to do.

That part of it was good. But it was no less backbreaking, so he did not stick with any job very long, always hoping he could find something easier to do and still make a decent wage or, God it would be nice, strike it rich somehow. Then he met up with Stan and the two rode together and got each other into and out of scrapes but never got rich, together or separate.

Now he had been chasing that damned boy for near a month and it was snowing instead of raining and he would be goddamned if he was going to let some kid get the best of him. Stan would be laughing at him if he could see how Corey had got himself into this thing. He began to wonder if Stan would have done the same thing for him. Sure he would. Stan was a real friend, and real friends stood up for each other no matter what.

He came to a cold campsite, dismounted, and checked it over. Couldn't be more than a few hours old. He scouted the sign. Two horses, all right, but they were headed in different directions. Blast them to hell! Which one was the boy? He tried to gauge the weight of the rider that was going west against the imprint of the tracks that followed the black trickle south toward the Gila. But the first horse was smaller and lighter than the second, so who could tell? It would take a tracker far more expert than Corey Logue. He exhausted every cuss word he had ever learned on this lousy situation. The trail was fresh. He was not far behind. But which way should he go?

One time he and Stan had faced a road that forked in two directions and they were hungry and needed work and had no idea in Hades which way to go. So Stan had proposed a solution: he would take the last coin they possessed and let Corey flip it. Heads meant they would ride in one direction, tails the other. So Corey had tossed it and it came up heads and that meant the upper fork and they had ridden it and found work before sundown and it seemed like a pretty good system at the time.

Corey fished out a ten-dollar cartwheel and decided heads would take him west, tails south toward the river. He flipped the coin over his head and it spun and fell to earth. Tails.

He had nothing to lose but time—and an abundance of that—so he remounted and pulled the horse around to follow the black streambed and wished he had something to eat because his belly was talking to him.

CHAPTER 9

The muscled claybank stepped easily through the fine snow, blowing steam from her nostrils. She was accustomed to Joel by now, and he gave her her head. The day unfolded before him in silent challenge, and the sky remained blank and threatening. He had never anticipated this: that time could move even more slowly than he had been used to in his tedious life at home. Without anything familiar to cling to, he had a single simple purpose. To stay alive.

By dusk the horse took him from the widening stream onto higher ground. The snow was not melting, but blew in misty waves across the flatness. The horse smelled the river ahead. Joel reined the animal to the west as they approached the Gila.

If he made it to Tucson, he must write to mother to tell her he was doing fine. He must not allow her to worry about him. He was hungry, having chewed on the dried beef to keep his stomach from sounding an alarm the entire desert could hear.

It rapidly grew colder and Joel felt his neck stiffen, his ears grow brittle. He must find shelter. As the sun fell he did not allow the tired mare to slacken her pace. The sky cleared and the moon rose. Across the silvered snow, shadows danced and there was the crunch of hoof. Joel sat stiffly, breathing hard. He needed sleep badly. But he had learned to get by with less sleep when he was riding with Henry.

So he held himself in the saddle, sore as hell, and rode on.

At first it was a faint flicker and he was not certain he had really seen it. He squinted, tried to focus on the source of the light.

The claybank snorted and tossed her head. She smelled something. Joel halted the horse, sucked in a lungful of bitterly cold air. Even though his nose was running he smelled it too. Smoke. He kneed the claybank forward.

A house: on the edge of a small wood it was set like a little box among the tall trees. Here the hills were rounder and lower, and he suspected there was a town nearby.

Joel screwed up the courage to approach. From the windows the light threw yellow squares on the snow. Someone was inside: he imagined a terrible old man who had not flinched in the face of Indian attacks in earlier years and who would not hesitate to kill this intruder. He thought of himself shot off the back of the horse and lying in the snow bleeding slowly to death. But he went forward.

Joel dismounted, ground hitched the claybank, and checked that the pistol was still at his hip. He took a few tentative steps closer, then called out.

"Hullo! Hullo!"

A shadow moved across the front window. But otherwise there was no reply, so he announced himself once again, remaining well away from the door in the comforting shadow of a tree. He waited.

A voice came through the window: "Who is out there?"

At first Joel thought it was a child. He said, "I am alone. I mean no harm. I would like a place to sleep tonight."

For what seemed like several minutes there was no reply. Then the unexpected voice said, "Show yourself."

Joel stepped from the shadow and stood about five yards from the door. The light from the window fell on his face. The door opened and more light flooded toward him. A figure limped into the light, emerged from the doorway, and the first thing Joel saw was a rifle aimed directly at his chest. He lifted his hands to show that he held no weapon.

"Closer." It was a woman's voice, no mistaking. Joel took two steps forward. "Stop." He could see now she was wearing a shawl, but he could not make out her face.

"My name is Joel Stark," he began, forgetting Henry's insistence that he use a false name.

"I don't care about that. You have a gun?"

"It's holstered."

"Give it over."

He remembered Henry's words of caution about keeping hold of this, his only protection. He made no move for the weapon. He said, "I don't plan to use it."

"Throw it down."

The voice was calm, firm in its demand. The silhouette did not move.

He unholstered the revolver. "Here it is." He tossed it at her feet.

She quickly scooped it inside. She stood erect. "You may come in now."

Joel went inside. It was very warm and bright and close. The scent of wax permeated the place; there were many candles burning, no kerosene lamps. The fireplace was dark. The house smelled of stewed meat and vegetables; a big pot sat on the stove. The woman closed the door behind him and he turned.

"You can look, but I'll do the talking," she said.

She was small. Violet eyes, wide and alert, a heart-shaped face, a softly pointed chin. Coppery hair cut short and pulled back over her ears, fastened with a ribbon. Her mouth opened only very slightly as she spoke. She stepped around him and pushed his gun away with her left foot. That was when he noticed the limp again: her right foot seemed unable to hold her weight. She did not let it hinder her as she pulled a chair from the table and indicated he should sit down. When he did she took a few steps back, holding the rifle on him.

"What makes you think you can ride in here and make yourself at home?"

"I only asked. This is the first place I have seen all day. I'm tired and hungry. I don't mean to be any trouble."

She examined him minutely. Henry's whiskeycolored eyes had probed him like this, learned everything about him in a very short time. This woman made him uncomfortable and he wished he had ridden on by.

"How do I know you won't kill me?"

Joel thought of the horse, at least as thirsty and hungry as he was. He said, "I'll sleep outside with the horse. If I could borrow an extra blanket—"

"I don't have an extra blanket. I don't even have firewood."

"I can fetch some, help you build a fire."

"I'm not asking for charity. You're the one needs help."

Joel rose, glanced at his revolver on the floor. "I won't bother you, ma'am. Maybe I better just keep moving."

She cocked her head in a funny way. The attitude reminded Joel of a ground squirrel with whom he had once tried to make friends.

"Stay put. You said you were hungry." She pushed herself upright and placed the rifle against the wall away from the stove. "I might as well trust you with that gun. If you're going to kill me, there's nothing I can do about it anyhow."

Joel did not pick up his gun. He said, "I'll get some firewood."

Outside it seemed much colder, after the closeness of the cabin. He unsaddled the claybank and picketed her.

He returned with an armful of dry sticks that the snow had not touched. He dropped them by the fireplace and asked the woman if he should build the fire.

"Make it a small one." She had the stove going pretty well and the house was adequately warm.

Joel did, and soon it was crackling bravely. He returned to the chair where he had sat earlier. He saw that his gun was on the table, not on the floor.

She served him a generous meal: a beef stew with potatoes and carrots and onions, warm bread smeared with strawberry jam, and a big mug of steaming coffee. She sat across from him as he ate. Neither spoke until he finished the last spoonful of stew and swallowed the last drop of coffee.

His stomach was stretched tight and his eyelids felt like lead. "That was a fine supper, ma'am. Saved my life."

"My name is Claire Thane," she said.

"Pleased to make your acquaintance. You know my name."

"Where are you headed, Joel?" she asked, friendlier, less afraid. Her small white hands lay flat on the tablecloth.

"I'm not rightly sure. I have to get to Tucson, but not for six or eight months. To meet someone and return the horse and saddle. They're both loans." Her eyes widened a fraction. "A real loan. From a man named Henry Root."

This meant nothing to her, but Joel wanted to say it, to give her the facts of the matter so that she would know he was not a horse thief. Her face became smooth again, less worried.

"You can put the horse in the shed out back. It's warmer in there. We used to have a horse . . ." She looked down at her hands.

"Thanks," Joel said. When he had put the horse in, watered her, and given her some grain, he came back into the cabin. Claire Thane had laid out a pallet between the stove and the fireplace. She had said she did not have an extra blanket. He did not ask her why she had changed her mind.

"You can sleep there," she said. Then she went to her room, a curtained-off section of the house that reminded Joel of his own.

He removed his boots. In the morning he would ask her where he might find a job around here.

CLAIRE THANE

She had been born that way, with the bad foot, and she had always been a small girl. The neighbors whispered that she had been cursed, that she was not supposed to have survived, that she carried the sign of God's disfavor. It had been difficult to learn to walk and painful to grow to womanhood with no friends.

He was thirty and she sixteen. He was a friend of her father's and had known Claire since she was a little girl. He never took much notice of her until she turned fifteen. Her golden hair grew in shiny curls and she combed it three times a day to keep it clean and maintain its luster. She combed it back from her pinkscrubbed face. She was shy and quiet and obeyed her mother and father and did her chores without complaint. Her violet eyes did not betray the rebellion that boiled in her heart.

When she turned sixteen, Frank Thane asked her father for her hand. Within six months they were married and Frank took her away to his property outside of town where he had built a cabin and a shed and kept a horse. He planned one day to clear the land and farm it.

Claire worked hard every day: cooking, laundry, keeping the house tidy for her husband. She learned what he liked to eat and what he did not like. He made his wishes clear. And in bed he took her when he wanted and left her alone when he did not want her, which was not very often in the first few years they were together.

But what of Frank Thane? He was decent enough. Yet he never had his feet on the ground. He had plans —many grand plans—and he told her about them and they sounded good, but nothing came of them. He spent a lot of time in town drinking with the other men. Sometimes he would not come home at night and she was lonely and wished he was there. What is the point of being married if your husband is not around?

Nothing panned out, and she often wondered where he got enough money to live on. She guessed that he gambled and was pretty good at it. He was always talking about getting a big stake together, and that was gambler's talk.

Frank Thane was a very big man with a head of curly black hair and great quantities of it all over the rest of his body. He wore a full beard all year round and allowed her to trim it every four months or so. She wanted him to look clean and presentable—for whatever business he conducted in town—so she kept his clothes washed and mended and ironed and as neat as possible since he sometimes slept in them for a few days running.

She never really knew him. They had been married for six years when Frank left to make a fortune as a prospector. One day he came home redeyed after several days away and smelling of whiskey and burning with gold fever. Said some friends of his were going to file a claim in a newly discovered field in New Mexico and it was now or never if he was ever going to be a rich man like he had always planned. He said, Pack my clothes and fix up some food to carry. She did, never questioning him but wanting to, wanting to say, You're crazy, Frank, why don't you find some steady work and try to build up something here. It would not have done any good.

So he was gone and Claire kept busy around the house and waited and wondered if she would ever see him again. He had been away for three months when she knew she was expecting a child. The sickness never abated: she awoke every morning with it and suffered through the day with it and knew it would be there the next day and it was. Her belly swelled only slightly, but enough to show that she was pregnant. Frank had taken the horse, so Claire had to walk the five miles to her parents' home in town. Her mother took her in and put her to bed. It was late autumn and cold and wet. Immediately, Claire knew something was wrong with the baby.

The next four weeks passed in a hellish blur: and on Christmas Eve she miscarried. She did not see the baby. Her mother buried it behind the house. It had been a boy. Her family said it would have been a cripple like Claire herself. She heard their whispers and, when she had recovered her strength, she went back to Frank's house to await his return.

Claire survived the winter and spring with supplies she had laid in when she learned she was pregnant. It was enough, barely, to keep her alive. And when it became warmer she planted a garden on the side of the house where Frank had begun his long-promised clearing of the land. She planted potatoes and vegetables and a small section of wheat and corn. With some money she had secreted for emergencies (she had, a few times, carefully looted Frank's pockets when he was sleeping off several days' debauchery), she bought a milk cow that grazed on the north side of the cabin and lived in the shed.

She had no contact with her family and she did not want to. She had a few books: the Bible, a copy of *Wuthering Heights,* an old waterlogged edition of *Oliver Twist,* some ladies' magazines that her mother had discarded. Not much, and she practically memorized every story in the magazines. In this way she waited for Frank Thane to come home.

He never did. And by the time she realized he never would, Claire had learned how to take care of her own needs.

I do not need a man, she told herself.

Every two or three weeks she walked into town to trade for food and supplies and kept herself going in this way. She still had a little money stored by for emergencies. And Frank had left an old rifle with a box of cartridges. She kept the gun cleaned and oiled, just in case. And she got along day by day and saw no one except on her trips to town and she liked it better that way. That way she could forget about her foot, which had never bothered her nor hampered her except when other folks made an issue of it. Frank had seen that it did not impede her and he had stopped talking about it soon after their marriage.

Sometimes she wondered where Frank Thane was,

if he was still alive or a bleached skeleton on a mountainside in Colorado or New Mexico. His face faded quickly from her memory, only the name and the legality of their marriage and a few fleeting remembrances of him coming home drunk and taking her and how she had kept herself from crying until he was gone the next day.

Once she quit crying, she was dry for a long time after. And she did not expect any man to look at her ever again.

CHAPTER 10

"You can stay here, rest awhile if you want," she said.

"Why did you change your mind about me?" Joel had not touched the Smith & Wesson since last night. It lay undisturbed on the table, an irreligious icon. Until he knew she did not feel threatened he would not pick it up.

"I didn't change my mind. I still don't know if I can trust you, but I want to."

Claire had laid out an ample breakfast for Joel: biscuits with bacon gravy, butter, strawberries, cream, fresh coffee. Two eggs were boiling on the stove. She served them in a blue bowl, and Joel cracked the shells, scooped out the hot eggs. She drank her coffee with cream. He wanted to talk, but did not know what to say. She fixed her eyes upon him, watched him eat. Her white elbows were planted on the checkered tablecloth.

He wanted to ask her where her husband was, why she was living here alone and unprotected. But he hadn't the nerve.

Finally he said, "I'll pay you back. There must be something I can do around the place."

"You don't owe me anything."

He sopped a piece of biscuit in the rich, salty gravy. Henry would be impressed by this spread. For a moment he almost forgot the privations of the trail, the stale taste of beef jerky and the hollow ache in his belly from hunger. It had been more than hunger, though. There had been fear and loneliness, aimless hours in the saddle, the not knowing what lay ahead in the next hour, the next day. Here at least was a reminder that there may still be the promise of something permanent and real—a house, a woman, a meal. Yet he did not belong here. He savored the taste of the egg.

"I'm going into town this morning to buy some supplies. Do you need anything?"

"No, thank you."

"I want you to make yourself at home, sleep some more if you want. I'll be gone for a few hours."

"How far is town?"

"Five miles."

"But you don't have a horse."

"No. I walk." Her eyes glittered defiantly. "I've done it for years," she said emphatically. Her small chin jutted forward, and she held her coffee cup firmly in both hands.

Joel did not question her further. It was clear that she was not used to answering to strangers. He concentrated on his meal.

She broke the awkward silence. "It's nice to have someone around for a change. It's so quiet out here, away from town. Are you finished?"

He nodded. She removed the plates from the kitchen table, stacked them in a water basin on the stove.

"May I take a bath when you're gone, ma'am?" He

forced the words out and immediately wanted to reclaim them.

But she said, "Sure. Fetch the tub in from the shed and I'll put some water on to heat."

Claire pulled on a pair of man's boots, a long coat, a woolen scarf, and a gray hat and left.

The bath cured Joel of his many aches and almost made him forget his troubles for an hour. The day had broken sunny. The snow was melting and the earth was turning black and green.

When he had dressed he took pen, ink, and paper from his bag and sat at Claire's table to write.

Dear Mother:

I finally have a chance to write, to tell you I am safe and you need not worry about me. It has been difficult for me since I left Lamont. I am not used to living "on the scout" as they say in novels, but I have been very fortunate to have encountered some people who have been very helpful to me.

But I miss you terribly, and I wish I had not had to run away before daddy was properly buried. Perhaps I should have stayed and faced those men, gone to the law. They should pay for what they did to daddy. One of them, I believe, is still following me.

When I first ran away I was scared, and I had no idea where I was going. Then I met a good man who helped me. His name is Henry Root, and he is a Negro. He loaned me a horse and a saddle and traded me a smaller gun for daddy's big revolver, which is too heavy for me to carry anyhow. The smaller pistol is all I should need.

Henry taught me a lot, most of all how to survive and not to give up when things are going poorly. If it weren't for him I'd probably be dead or starving by now.

I am staying at the house of a woman who has allowed me to sleep here in exchange for work around the place. Her husband is dead, I think, so she is alone too. I feel sorry for her, yet she seems to get along fine on her own. I won't be here long, since she is unable to pay me for the work I do, and I think I am more a burden than a help to her. But she's been very kind to me.

I had not expected it to be so cold this time of year. I remember on the day daddy and I went into Lamont it was warm and I expected spring had arrived for good, but the rain came, then later the snow and it was like winter again, cold and mean. Summer seems a long way off. I have not felt the warmth of the sun since daddy died.

I think about you all the time, hoping you are well and do not hurt too much. It cannot ever be the same again—and I do not know whether I will see you again. But if there is any way to do so, I will. When I find myself a paying job I will send you money. Eventually I must reach Tucson to meet Henry Root and return his horse and saddle.

> Your loving son,
> Joel Stark

Claire returned, carrying a heavy box of food and other provisions—a staggeringly large burden for such a small woman to handle. Joel helped her store the supplies in the cabinets that lined the kitchen wall. When he reached for a can of sugared fruit his fingers brushed her hand.

He pulled his hand away and did not look at her.

Claire said, "What's wrong?"

"Sometimes I think I'm carrying a curse. I don't want to put it on anyone else. And your husband—"

"Is that why you're afraid of me?"

"I'm not afraid of you."

"Yes, you are."

When he did not answer, she challenged him: "It is because I'm a woman."

"It's not that. I don't know what it is."

"Let me tell you something, Joel. You're not cursed. You're no different from me or anyone else. Maybe you have had bad fortune, but so have many others."

"Death is following me. I feel it. That's why I can't touch you."

Haltingly at first, Joel told her how his father had been killed, how he had shot a man, how he was running for his life. He thought there was a man following him.

Claire listened without interrupting his story. When he finished, she said: "There is no reason behind any of this. It just happened."

"That can't be. There has to be a reason," he argued.

"You've seen very little of the world. I was already married a year when I was your age."

"I wanted to be a priest," Joel said quietly, sharing his secret for the first time.

"And you've changed your mind because of all this?"

"It doesn't seem important now."

"Joel, don't give up your ambitions because of what happened to your father." She touched his hand. "And don't be afraid of other people. I have lived with that fear for a long time. It's no good."

"What happened to your husband?" Joel asked.

Claire recited the story as if it had happened to another person. She said: "Whether he is dead or alive, he is dead to me now."

"Do you want me to build a new fire?"

"Yes. It's getting cold." She held the woven shawl to her shoulders. She watched as he laid the kindling, stacked wood on top, and applied a sulphurhead match. The kindling snapped, caught, and burst into flame. Quickly the dry logs ignited.

Joel stood back and admired the fire. At least there was something he could do right. Behind him, Claire noticed the letter he had written to his mother. She scanned it quickly, then put it down before he turned around and came back to his chair.

"Aren't you lonely living by yourself out here?"

"Yes," Claire said.

"Why don't you move into town?"

"Nothing for me there."

"At least there are people around."

"I don't need people. They feel uncomfortable

around me because of my foot. At least Frank never concerned himself with that. I kept his house clean and warmed his bed. That was all that mattered. Other folks expect too much."

The fire singed their faces as they stared directly into it. Outside the sun had fallen behind the trees. There was not a sound except for the sizzle of the logs and their own voices.

"I used to feel that I would never fit in, wherever I went. Mother and daddy were always quarreling. In school I never had any real friends. I still feel that way. I don't know what I expected it to be like to grow up. I suppose I'll find out."

Claire studied Joel's face. Beneath the unkempt red hair the blue eyes reflected the glow of the fire and seemed to catch the heat too.

"Where will you go?" she asked.

"I don't know. Find work someplace."

"Come here, Joel."

He stood before her.

"You are a nicelooking boy. And you will make a fine man, a good husband and father. I want you to know I truly mean that."

He felt a shiver. She looked beautiful to him. He had never been so close to a woman. So damnably close.

He lifted her into his arms and kissed her.

JOEL STARK

Your nocturnal imaginings had not prepared you for it. Nothing could have. Daddy had once attempted to tell you how it was between men and women, but he got tonguetied and embarrassed. He never finished his explanation. He did say something that made a lasting impression on you: When you get to be a man, big boy, it won't be all of a sudden, but gradual. It will happen when you aren't expecting it, and you can't wish too hard for it.

You supposed he meant that for all your planning and praying and hoping and worrying, you could not control a damn thing—least of all a woman's heart.

When they had ended she said: I have not been with a man since Frank left me.

I have never been with a woman before.

You were very considerate.

What to say? How to answer her? Finally, you said: I hope I didn't hurt you.

You didn't.

She gently touched your face in the darkness behind the curtain in her bed and her fingers were warm and soft and charged with emotion.

You reached for her, took her shoulders in your hands and she felt small and soft and you kissed her again.

You've been good to me.

A warm ripple of laughter, not cruel, with a kiss as an antidote.

I'm not being kind, Joel. I'm taking as much from you as I'm giving. You must learn that about women. We are not the pure, saintly creatures you want to make us. We can be selfish and hurtful and bad—even someone like me who has few opportunities to be anything at all. I am glad you came here.

What would you have done if I had never come by?

I don't know. Gone on like always. There's nothing else to do. Until you die—and that's the end of all the worry.

You don't believe in God?

I used to. Nothing that has happened to me for the past ten years makes any sense if God had anything to do with it. Without Him hovering at my shoulder I can see things more clearly and accept what comes my way. Like you.

She smiled and held your hand.

I don't know what to believe anymore, you said. I used to think there was nothing greater than to serve God.

In the light of a single candle you could see her moist eyes.

She said: What has happened can't be erased, Joel. Your father, the killings. All of that is past. But, don't you see, it's not all bad. Maybe you can build something from it.

You turned from her and closed your eyes and fought for sleep, which did not come for a long time.

*   *   *

A bright, warm day in October. It comes back to you with painful brilliance. The house is quiet. Surrounded by trees that are shedding their leaves in showers of gold and brown and red, carpeting the grass. The leaves crackle when you walk through them. The air is brittle, delicious. Yet the peace and warmth will not last. Soon winter will overwhelm this delicate balance with indiscriminate violence.

Daddy calls you, and you run to him.

He explains to you how it works, how careful you must be, how you must keep it cleaned and oiled, how deadly a matter a gun is.

His long fingers nimbly manipulate the Colt's Walker. To you it might as well be a rifle. But you are just a kid of ten who asked daddy to show you how to shoot. Remember the smile that had passed swiftly over his grave face? He waited until mother was out of the house, delivering some sewing in town.

You can see daddy's white, strongly muscled forearms, the pelt of black hair encroaching onto the back of his hands. The red knuckles and long fingers with yellow nails, the fingertips stained by tobacco. He tosses away a cigar and inspects the gun with narrowed eyes, then dips onto his haunches.

Take it in both hands, big boy. It's heavy, but easy to get used to. Feel the balance. Hold it like this—

He molds your fingers around the grip, steadies the barrel.

The first time you fire it, the infernal thing kicks you back five feet and deafens you. Your feet are shocked out from under you. Daddy laughs goodnaturedly and picks you up.

He says: Powerful weapon. Just have to get used to it.

The next time he crouches behind you and helps you hold it up, and when you fire he is there to support you against the recoil.

It comes back to you, something you can never forget: falling back against his chest, his arms around your shoulders, the warmth of his breath in your ears, the smell of his perspiration, the scratch of his whiskers on your cheek. You want to stay there in his arms forever.

Mother doesn't have to know about this, big boy. She might not like it, he says.

Why not?

I know what she doesn't like. She wouldn't want me teaching you how to shoot. That's the way she is. So let's keep it between us.

A conspiracy among men. You promise not to say anything to her. Guns are a man's business.

CHAPTER 11

For about three weeks Joel practiced with the Smith & Wesson .45. He practiced more for accuracy than speed, drawing cold, aiming steady, and firing calm and quick. Beyond Claire's shed was a clearing about fifty yards long and twenty yards wide. Joel stood at one end and shot at the paper target he had pinned to a dead tree on the other end. He was there three hours in the morning, three hours in the afternoon. It became a natural, unthinking function for him, like breathing.

Claire said nothing to him about it. She bought another box of two hundred cartridges for him to practice with. At first she winced at every shot that punctured the stillness she cherished, then she got used to it, to the sound of the shots, if not to the boy's having his own motives for learning.

Joel had torn up the letter to his mother and re-written it several times. It always came out the same, and he decided to send it to her. Claire said she would post it the next time she went into town. When she left that day Joel was out back practicing. The crack of gunfire echoed through the morning. He went about his unvarying routine, taking each position, one after another, like an automaton. The milk cow shifted impatiently, but even she was accustomed to the noise by now.

Joel had lost at least a dozen pounds since his flight from Lamont. And now he was eating even less at Claire's table. Perhaps, he told himself, because he was in love. He tried to put her out of his mind as he practiced, but it was not so easy. He felt responsible for her. She was a part of him now. He had not expected these sudden complications.

This puzzled him, as he reloaded the revolver and took a new position ten feet to the left to gain a different angle on the target.

So many contradictory ideas were battling in his head. What if her husband were not dead after all? What if Claire became with child? What if he was being dishonest with her and himself? When he was with her, Joel knew what he and Claire had was good —but when he was alone he was tugged by doubts. He had to find work and meet up with Henry in Tucson.

Joel half cocked and broke the revolver open, emptied the chambers, inserted more bullets, and swung the cylinder shut again. Six loads. He holstered the gun and moved twenty paces closer to the target. His feet well apart, his body tensed and balanced, he drew and fired three quick shots. Then he walked to his right, repeating the three-shot pattern. His nose filled with the smell of burned powder and he forgot Claire and his father and everything else for a few minutes.

He ejected the used shells and reloaded. He replaced the tattered target and started again with his practice routine. In this way he used up sixty rounds within two hours. Even taking his time, he was using up ammunition at a rapid rate. He hoped Claire would bring another box back from town. His shoulder and back muscles ached so he rested briefly, sitting on a tall stump.

He closed his eyes. God, I feel like an old man sometimes.

Claire returned before noon. She had ridden the claybank at Joel's insistence, which saved her hours of walking. As he attended to the horse, she went inside without a word. When he finished, he went in and found her sitting at the table, her hands clasped tightly. Something was wrong.

She held out the letter addressed to Eleanor Stark. "I didn't post it. I couldn't."

He touched her shoulder. "What happened?"

"I went to buy another box of cartridges for you. In the store there was a man. He was buying bullets too. I heard him talking to the clerk, and to some other men. He was asking about you by name. He wanted to know if anybody had seen you."

Joel sat down on the chair next to her. His heart pounded against his chest like a mailed fist. "What did he say about me?"

"He said you had killed five men up in Lamont and he was deputized to bring you back to stand trial."

"It's a lie. He's one of the riders who shot daddy. He's after me because I shot a friend of his."

"I know, Joel. I bought the cartridges and tried to stay clear of him. But he saw me as I was leaving, stopped me. He said, 'You seen this boy, lady?' I said I hadn't but I would keep an eye out for him. He said, 'You better. He's a dangerous gunny if there ever was one.' I said thank you. He looked at me as if he *knew*. But he didn't follow me. He couldn't know."

Joel said, "I wonder why it took him this long to get here. If he followed Henry . . ." He shuddered. "He couldn't have gone all the way to Tucson—maybe he changed his mind halfway there, or maybe he just took his time following my sign down here."

"I don't care how long it took him. You've got to get out of here. He'll come by the place sooner or later. You can't be here when he does."

"I won't leave you, Claire."

"Don't be stupid. If you stay here it will be bad trouble for me too."

Joel grasped her arms. "Come with me."

"No. I can't leave this place."

He slapped the table angrily and she started. "Then I'll stay. I can help you work the land. If I hide out while this man is in town—"

"It won't work, Joel."

He turned to her, struggling to control the tears, and she was looking at him with those strange violet eyes and he could tell she wanted him. He wanted her. She was all he had.

At sundown the red disk met the gray earth and all things quickened at the approach of night.

After supper they sat near the fire, Joel in the rocking chair, Claire in her sewing chair. They said little.

He was tired but did not want to sleep anymore. He just wanted to stay with her.

The thought came to him and he blurted it out: "Claire, will you marry me?"

"Why in heaven's name would you want to marry a widow woman like me?" She did not look up from her needlepoint.

"You know why."

"You're still only seventeen. What we have had does not prove that we should be married. Don't make it more difficult than it already is, Joel."

"If you hadn't run into that man, if he wasn't any-place near here—would it be different then?"

"I can't say. Quit torturing yourself over it."

"I can't get it out of my head."

"You'll have to. I don't want you to get yourself killed." She glanced up at him, dropping her hands to her lap. "Promise me you'll be very careful. I don't know what I'd do if I heard anything happened to you."

Joel stood. Long shadows lay upon the cabin floor. He braced himself against a window and gazed out. The trees whispered conspiratorially in the soughing wind. He saw nothing but bleakness out there.

She resumed her needlework. "Don't think it over too hard."

"No matter how hard I think, it doesn't help," he conceded.

"You're an intelligent young man. You should go to college."

"That's what mother and daddy always wanted. They thought I should be a lawyer. They made a lot of sacrifices for me. I never realized it until all this happened."

Claire said, "Come here. Don't stand over there."

He moved away from the window, knelt in front of her, his face uplifted to hers.

"I don't understand what's happening, what's the point."

She touched the side of his head, ran her fingers along his jaw line, held his chin. This boy had brought something new into her life: he had awakened in her the capacity to give of herself. His youth and his vulnerability were qualities she could not expect to find in a fullgrown man. This is how he touched her, and why she could not hold him to her and keep him here, why she could not tell him all that was in her heart.

"There is no point, Joel, except that you must do what you have to do to survive. I don't know why you rode in here, why I let you stay, why you didn't kill me, why I didn't shoot you. I do know I am glad that you are here now."

"I could stay with you always." He remained on his knees before her. "Why can't I stay?"

"It is simply impossible."

"But, Claire—"

"I don't mean to be cruel. It hurts me to say it."

"It's all a goddamn lie."

"No, my dear, it is the only truth we can ever know. Now you must shut up about it."

He thought he should kiss her, and he did. Her breath mingled with his and both were finished talking.

PART III

MONTGOMERY G. STAINBACK

San Mateo was his town; he had created it from virtually nothing and shaped it in his own image. Now it was a center of enormous profit from thriving mines and cattle operations. Townsfolk borrowed from his banks and spent their money at his general mercantile, at his saloons, and in the plush crib he had built over at the west end and imported talent for—talent from St. Louis and New Orleans, all of them topdollar girls who paid him fifty percent of their gross earnings. He owned every square foot in town and thousands of acres around. He owned the mayor and the marshal and the marshal's deputy. He had financed the rail spur that took his silver and copper and cows to Eastern markets and brought him money and more men and women to populate San Mateo, to work and earn and spend. What a glorious cycle, a providential mechanism, a part of the very Natural Order which had put the minerals in the mountains a thousand millennia ago!

But metaphysics was not Stainback's strong suit. His mind worked best on a day-by-day, dollar-by-dollar basis. He planned in minute detail, down to the last penny spent and earned, and he kept it all in his head, and God it felt good to know he was one of the richest men in the territory and ahead lay more of the same.

Ambitious, slavedriving, profane, even greedy some would say. But they were pious churchgoers who could see no farther than their noses, which were always buried in Bible verses anyhow. His reply was how else was life supposed to be lived? That was one of the few questions he ever posed—to himself or anyone else. He knew no other way. He was what everybody—those who respected him and those who hated him—called a big man. Twenty-four carats. To him bigger was better; the smaller would be swallowed or driven out or driven under; and that was the way it should be.

Growing up in St. Joe, young Stainback never knew his father, who had deserted his mother soon after his birth. She lived with her brother and sister-in-law, Ellman and Margaret, who never let her forget the "tragedy" of her marriage. The boy felt Aunt Margaret's condescension, and the back of her hand, from an early age. A heavy boy, with sloping shoulders and a large head and oversized hands and feet, he was never allowed a moment's leisure for there were always chores to be done, and he paid for his room and board in a thousand humiliating ways. But he suffered silently with his mother who kept to her own room most of the time. He never talked back to Aunt Margaret, never failed to obey her slightest or silliest command.

Uncle Ellman felt the sting of her tongue as frequently as the youth, and he sympathized with

Stainback though there was little he could do to ease the boy's passage. He took him into his print shop as an apprentice and taught him the craft. Ellman was not a master; he had not the eye nor the ambition to do any but contract jobs. He hired his time indiscriminately and for less money than competitors in St. Joe. Thus he made a marginal living, never "getting ahead," as Aunt Margaret urged. But you can't change a rock, she always said, frustrated but determined never to give up on her impossible charges.

Stainback was little use as a printer but a wizard with the ledger books. With his affinity for ciphering and his sense of what was possible beyond the dull and demeaning existence Aunt Margaret represented, he took to the quill and paper like a bear to refuse: no one else wanted it and he craved it.

As keeper of the purse for Uncle Ellman he learned quickly that a dollar here and there every week would not be missed. He began to accumulate a private stake. He dreamed of freedom from the dreary routine of the shop and from the stifling house where Aunt Margaret reigned like a dowager. But more than dream, he planned.

On his twentieth birthday he recovered the cache of paper and silver currency from a locked desk in the print shop. More than five hundred dollars. He was not rich, but it was a damn fine beginning. He left his mother fifty dollars pinned to a note and fled on the railroad train from Missouri to Omaha.

Almost thirty years later he was the big man in San Mateo, getting bigger every day.

                    * * *

I don't understand what you're telling me, Blue,
Stainback said, stifling a yawn.

It was not even sunup and the old drunk had
busted into his house asking for him, said he had to
save the boss's life. A kid with the lightnin'est draw I
ever see'd, the drunken prospector had said.

Stainback sat up in his wide deep bed beneath a
brocaded canopy supported by four tall oaken posts.
He wore a silk nightshirt that generously allowed for
his paunch. A balding, bigboned man with blue bags
under his eyes. The room itself was high and long
with a big window open to the east that admitted a
vague mauve light onto the carpeted floor.

Dahlgren felt lost amid such affluence. Like I told
you, Mr. Stainback, the kid's here and he said he's
lookin' for you.

You'll have to start over, Dahlgren. I'm not awake
yet.

Stainback signaled to the tall man by the
doubledoored entrance to the master bedroom, his
newly hired bodyguard. He said: Logue, have Omar
bring me some coffee.

The man, who wore a lefthand belt gun and a
twelve-inch knife on the right side, slipped out of the
room.

Now tell it to me straight—from the beginning,
Stainback said to Dahlgren.

The old man said Kid Stark was in town gunning
for the top man—aimed to make himself the boss in
San Mateo. He told Stainback about the kid's fast
draw, only in the telling the fry pan became a rattle-

snake that had crawled into Blue's shack behind the visitor. According to Dahlgren, the kid already had shot six men dead up in Lamont, the law was on his tail, and he was running scared but still wanted to show how mean he was so he was going to take the town down with him. The kid had a dangerous look in his eyes, Blue said, like the snake had just before young Stark had emptied his revolver into it.

Omar, the cook, arrived with the coffee on a silver tray inlaid with ivory. Logue was standing by the door again, listening silently. Blue Dahlgren's tale began to sink in.

Through the window Stainback could see the day being born crimson. He did not like the sound of what was coming out of Blue's mouth.

He asked for you, Mr. Stainback—by name. He's a gunny and I ain't lyin'.

No one has accused you of anything, Dahlgren.

The old man looked at him through liquid eyes. The ragged beard needed a good washing.

Thank you for the information, the boss said.

Just doin' my job, Blue added with a hopeful smile.

Stainback reached into his night table and pulled out a wad of greenbacks. He peeled off a bill and tossed it at Dahlgren. Here. Go out and get drunk. And stay out of trouble.

Sure, Mr. Stainback. Thanks, Mr. Stainback. Then Dahlgren was gone.

Montgomery Stainback called Corey Logue over to the bed. The man moved deliberately. He had been in town less than a week, having shown up at Stainback's door looking for work. He had agreed to

serve as a bodyguard until something better came
along. He had earned the boss's trust for his quiet
ways.

You ever heard of this Kid Stark? Stainback asked
him.

Logue thought for a moment before he spoke. He
said: Yeah, I heard of him. Up north. He killed some
people like the old man said. I heard of him.

Well, I don't like any of it. You get yourself over to
the marshal's office. Have him deputize you. Tell him
I said so. If the kid shows his face in town he's dead.
But I want it done legal.

Logue went wordlessly to his task.

Stainback pulled away the bed clothes and got up
to dress. He opened his wardrobe and paused to consider the dozens of suits he owned. He smiled to
himself. He would wear his black suit and a black tie.
Looked like there was going to be a funeral before
the day was done and he wanted to be dressed
proper.

Once fastened into his clothes, he stepped to the
mirror to comb his black hair smoothly back. A but-
ton popped from his vest. He bent to pick it up and
another jumped free. He stood upright with a grunt.

He went to the bureau and opened the top drawer.
He removed an old U.S. Army–issue .44 and a box of
shells. When the gun was loaded he stuck it in his
belt. It felt cold even through a double layer of clothing and pressed against the side of his belly like a
steel tumor.

This was a peaceful town and it was going to stay

that way. Who was this Kid Stark anyway? Sounded as though he had killed his way to quite a reputation. No, it wouldn't do to have him walk into San Mateo and start trouble.

CHAPTER 12

Far to the northwest was the Chiricahua reservation at San Carlos. There Nana, Geronimo, and the sons of Victorio, Cochise, and the other great war chiefs were wards of the government. When they had surrendered to General Crook a year ago, a defeated people, they had given up little, but today they had even less. On the barren reservation they attempted to live with honor, but they would not sit much longer and starve. Before they were too weak they would fight again. That was what Henry Root had said.

Joel remembered the Indians who had attended mass at Father Orosco's mission. They were Navajo, at one time a fierce, warloving people who had dominated the region over the scattered, nomadic Apache clans. The Navajo, after a brief, bloody resistance, had been quicker than other Indians to adopt the ways of the white man, and since then they had declined in number and strength. The women who came to Father Orosco's church wore heavy blankets on their heads in winter and summer, their faces darkly hidden.

He had been afraid of them. All his life he had heard stories of Indian savagery and depravity, of bizarre pagan customs and torture rites. But today as

he awoke upon the hillside with the sun glaring
boldly in his face and his back against the cold earth,
he understood what Father Orosco had once told
him.

"They are God's children. They could not have
known of His Son until the Church brought the Gospel to this land. They love their sons and daughters
just as white people love their own children. Their
ways are strange because they have never been
taught the truth. That is why I am here, to bring
them into the bosom of Holy Mother Church."

Father Orosco himself was born of mestizo stock in
Mexico. He knew what he was talking about. Yet was
that as far as it went? What about those thousands of
Indians who had died before the oncoming white
men, who had never had the chance to know the
truth of the Church? There was no justice in that.

This Joel had finally come to see for himself: there
was no justice in the affairs of men. Justice was imper-
sonal, distant, in some cases unobtainable. It mattered not that he had believed in a wise, patient,
forgiving God. The doors to the Great Tribunal were
closed to him.

Perhaps they would open today, perhaps they
would remain forever shut. He would not know before the day ended. He was starting from scratch in a
new town, with a frail hope, with a loaned horse and
a traded gun and his wits. He would begin again. It
was all he could do.

He was on Blue Dahlgren's hill. The dew on the
sparse grass cooled the steady breeze that blew from

the east against the ridge line that shimmered pinkly on the near horizon.

He broke his cold camp, washed his face in a swiftmoving stream, and saddled the claybank. As he cinched the saddle around the animal's belly fear gripped him. No reason behind it. For a moment he wondered if he should forget about San Mateo and Stainback and the job. Then he shrugged it off. He was just hungry; he had not had a decent meal in days. That was it.

He knocked on the door to the shack and stepped inside. No sign of Blue Dahlgren. Maybe the old man had business in town. Perhaps he had wandered off to get a head start on the day's drinking. Well, Dahlgren had already told him about Stainback.

Joel sat back in the saddle and let the horse negotiate the steep terrain. Soon they were in the valley and the hills had flattened and there was an apron of grass to cross and the promise of water and feed when the journey was done.

After two miles Joel reached the outskirts of San Mateo. It was all adobe and brick and wood, without much shape or reason to it. Everything was new, yet somehow shabby. A few taller structures stood out: probably the hotels and banks and the whorehouse Blue Dahlgren had so precisely enumerated in his inventory of Stainback's interests. Joel reined up to take in the layout.

At first glance it seemed little different from Lamont, which he knew so well, or a dozen other places he had ridden through since leaving home: unpainted watering holes, terminals of civilization lost among the weeds and dwarfed by the thrusting mountains. He wanted very badly to see a big brassy city like St. Louis or San Francisco, places he had read about and might now have a chance to see if he got a good job and saved enough money and made sure mother was taken care of. Maybe he could go back to Claire, when he had a stake and had grown up some. She would marry him and they would move to California or someplace and start fresh.

His eyes ranged up the sere street as he approached, the claybank taking measured steps into this unknown place. There were a few people out, but they paid the young stranger no mind.

The sun was well up now, throwing blunted shadows on the white dust that blew uneasily across the street. San Mateo was a skeleton and there was an unnatural quietness here.

Joel wanted to ask one of the men in the street where Mr. Stainback might be found, but as he approached the man averted his eyes and walked away.

So he dismounted and tied his horse in front of a barber shop and continued on foot. He watched his shadow precede him and realized he must have sprouted an inch or two in the past few months.

At the end of the block was an adobe box with a barred window and a reinforced door. The hand-painted sign overhanging the door said: MARSHAL-JAIL. He hesitated.

Henry Root had advised him not to use his real name because news of the killings in Lamont had spread throughout the territory. But he had already revealed his identity to Blue Dahlgren, who had in-

deed heard of his troubles. Chances were, others in
San Mateo, including the law, were aware of Joel
Stark too. Maybe it would be better to avoid the
marshal for now. He wished he had not told the old
man his name.

He was bothered by Blue's reaction last night to
the name and to the gun. It was silly, but he remembered the look on the man's face: fear and—something else. The recognition of an opportunity?

Joel started back toward his horse. Again he
thought, San Mateo was not for him, nor was Montgomery Stainback. He would find work elsewhere,
maybe in New Mexico. The claybank stood patiently
near the rail and lifted her head as Joel came closer.

He heard the heavy door creak open behind him.
He turned. Out stepped a man with a law badge
pinned to his chest. Besides the star, Joel saw the gun
belt and the bighandled knife. The man also wore a
gray Stetson, and Joel stopped and spoke to him.

"You the marshal?"

Corey Logue stared mutely at the youth. Joel
asked again and this time Logue said, "Deputy."

"Then maybe you can help me. I'm looking for Mr.
Stainback. Thought there might be some work."

Logue was breathing unaccountably hard. He
pushed back the hat brim. "No work for you."

The sun beat into the man's eyes, making him
squint uncomfortably, and Joel looked more closely.
He thought he had seen the face before but could not
pin it to a time or place. Crazily, he thought about
Claire's lost husband and wondered if maybe, im-
probably . . . then he remembered. He knew.

"What's your name?"

"What the hell does it matter?"

Joel stood only ten yards from the other. He backed up three paces. The deputy stood rooted to the step. Behind him, the open door revealed the black interior of the marshal's office and no sign of anybody inside.

The street was white, the deputy's face red, and Joel felt the heat of the sun between his shoulder blades. He tugged at the sweatstained bandanna around his neck. Then at the edge of his vision there was movement. To his left.

A man in a black suit stepped out of the building across the street. This man was looking right at him and opened his coat. Behind the black suit a third man stumbled into the glare. Joel recognized Blue Dahlgren and thought the old man had come in for a drink after all. For an instant Joel was relieved to see a familiar face among these strange ones.

Blue Dahlgren saw Joel at the same time and stopped in his tracks, a bottle dangling from his fingers. "It's him!" he said, then dove back into the tavern.

The black suit and the deputy did not pay any attention to Blue's clumsy antics. They concentrated on Joel. He took another step backward.

Logue said, "You killed Stan."

Joel took his revolver from the smooth holster. Logue was already aiming as Joel fired.

Logue crumpled into himself, the cocked weapon in his red fist. He made no sound as he hit the street.

Joel wondered what the hell was going on. The .45

was still warm in his hand, powder stink in his nostrils. Then he remembered the black suit. Just as he turned to locate it, a charge exploded in his ears and a bullet ripped through his rib cage. His lungs burned as he tried to breathe.

He stood long enough to steady the gun barrel and fire a single shot at Stainback. He was certain he had found his target and remembered the paper pinned to the tree behind Claire's house.

Joel fell. He thought he was dead but knew it could not be. Blood leaked through a hand pressed to the wound. He rolled onto his back, his clothing dust-smeared and incarnadine, and looked into the face of the sun that blinded him, but he did not want to close his eyes. With cold fingers he felt for mother's rosary in his vest pocket. The bandanna was soaked with perspiration and seemed to tighten around his neck.

Why, God? The question formed on his cracked lips.

Stainback had taken Joel's bullet above the heart and he too lay dead in the street, his shirt black with blood.

Blue Dahlgren came outside when the shooting was over, joining the crowd that gathered in the street. The marshal lumbered out of the tavern where he had been playing cards while three men died. The people looked at the bodies. Stainback everyone knew, and some had seen Logue around town during the past week, but the kid with the red hair whose body already seemed shriveled and old in the sun was a mystery.

The marshal hitched his belt and spoke first. "Anybody know the boy?" He scanned the faces of the onlookers.

"I do." Blue Dahlgren pushed forward, holding his bottle. "It's Kid Stark."

BLUE DAHLGREN

In later years—though not too many were left to him
—Blue Dahlgren told the story of Kid Stark to anyone who at least pretended to listen.

How the kid had snuck up to Blue's shack in the
middle of the night and got grub and whiskey at
gunpoint. The kid hadn't eaten proper in weeks and
he tore into it like a starved wolf. How he'd drunk the
whiskey and bragged that he'd nail Montgomery
Stainback because he was the biggest man around
and nobody deserved to be that rich. Stainback was
keeping the people down and the kid was determined to set accounts straight.

Blue enjoyed telling how the kid hated Stainback
so bad and how Stainback was too wide for his own
britches.

And Blue never forgot to mention his own role in
the drama: how he had run to town to warn
Stainback who had dismissed the idea of some kid
threatening him but stuck a gun in his belt before he
went out, just in case. If only the biggest man in the
county had listened to old Blue he would be alive
today—maybe.

"Ya gotta remember the kid was fast," Blue Dahlgren explained patiently, like a teacher with a partic-
ularly dull class. "I seen him shoot the eyes off a

rattlesnake over on my hill. He was good and he could of took Stainback easy in a fair fight. But there wasn't nothing fair about how they burned the kid. Two on one like that. He'd already killed ten men before he rode into San Mateo. He was just startin' out on his career and he was real young and nobody could of stood up to him alone. That's a fact."

ABOUT THE AUTHOR

Greg Tobin grew up in Independence, Missouri, attended Grinnell College, and graduated from Yale University. He is the author of several western novels, including *Steelman's Way* and *Jericho*. He lives with his wife and two sons in Irvington, New Jersey.